Christmas Victim

Jane Blythe

Bear Spots Publications
Melbourne Australia

Paperback
ISBN-13: 978-0-6484033-8-8

Cover designed by QDesigns

I'd like to thank everyone who played a part in bringing this story to life. Particularly my mom who is always there to share her thoughts and opinions with me. My awesome cover designer, Amy, who whips up covers for me so quickly and who patiently makes every change I ask for, and there are usually lots of them! And my lovely editor Mitzi Carroll, and proofreader Marisa Nichols, for all their encouragement and for all the hard work they put into polishing my work.

DECEMBER 20TH

10:49 P.M.

Why did her cat insist on having to go outside to do her business?

Why couldn't she use a litter box like every other cat?

No matter how hard she tried, Savannah Watson had not been able to train the cat to use the litter box, and she'd had Sequin since she was a kitten. Five years now and still no success, and for some reason Sequin insisted on making one last bathroom stop for the night before they went to bed.

So here she was in her pajamas, wrapped up in a blanket and sitting in her wheelchair waiting for Sequin to find just the right spot to go so they could go back inside and off to bed. Apparently, just any place wasn't okay; the silly cat had to find the perfect spot before she would go and was prancing around the yard like she didn't have a care in the world.

Sequin was lucky she loved her. The cat had been her little lifesaver these last few years. All the times she'd spent stuck in the house because sometimes it was just easier than trying to get out and about, the cat had kept her company. When she was lonely and stuck in despair, she would cuddle the animal close and cry into her soft fur. During the day, Sequin's favorite spot to nap was curled up on her lap. At night she continued to stay close by, as though she somehow knew that it was what Savannah needed. The constant purring had become one of the few things that truly soothed her.

Savannah shivered—it was so cold out tonight.

Where was Sequin?

It wasn't like the cat to take this long to do her business. Before bed she usually just popped outside, chose a spot to go in, then she was every bit as ready to snuggle under the covers as Savannah was. In fact, her cat was usually so quick that the only reason she came outside with her at all was because if she didn't, Sequin just stood on the back doorstep and meowed. It was like if she was going to suffer coming out into the cold night, then her owner had to as well.

Starting to feel a tiny prick of worry, Savannah wheeled away from the door and out into the yard. Had something happened to Sequin? She hadn't heard anything, but maybe the cat had fallen or been bitten by something—or maybe someone had snatched her.

"Sequin," she called as she scanned the yard. It was a dark night, the cloud cover was thick, cutting out most of the moon's glow. A little light spilled out from inside the house, but the farther she got from the door, the less illumination it gave. At least it wasn't snowing; that was one saving grace. Savannah hated everything to do with winter—everything but Christmas. And even that had lost its gloss the last couple of years.

Where was the cat?

She was getting annoyed now.

She was tired and in pain, and she just wanted to take some painkillers and go to sleep.

"Sequin," she hissed again, trying to keep her voice quiet. The new couple who'd moved in next door was very light sleepers, and she always tried to make sure she was as quiet as could be when she and Sequin were outdoors at night. On more than one occasion in the last four weeks since they'd moved in, she had woken them up. Their master bedroom was right next to Sequin's favorite patch of grass, and whenever she and the cat made too much noise, without fail, their light would switch on.

"Sequin," she called one last time. If the cat was going to ignore her, she was going to bed. It wouldn't hurt Sequin to be locked out for one night. There was a cat door leading into the garage so she could get indoors and keep warm.

"Last chance." Savannah gave her cat another opportunity to show herself.

When the little pest still stubbornly remained hidden, she turned her wheelchair around and headed back toward the house.

She hadn't gone more than a yard or so when she froze.

What was that?

Her brow furrowed in concentration.

It sounded like a muted bang.

A gunshot?

No.

That couldn't be right.

Could it?

Had she just imagined it?

It must be just a figment of her over-active imagination. She didn't like the dark, much less being outside in it. Outside and alone. Psychological scars lasted longer than physical ones, and were often harder to deal with.

With her ears still straining, listening for the tiniest of sounds, Savannah headed back for the house.

Then froze again as another muffled shot pierced the quiet night.

That was definitely a gunshot.

And it was coming from the Fishers' house.

Savannah didn't know a lot about the family besides the fact that one or both of the couple were light sleepers. Gavin and Violet Fisher were maybe five to ten years older than her, in their early or midthirties. They had two kids, twelve-year-old twins, a boy and a girl. The whole family seemed nice. Gavin had gotten Sequin down for her when the cat got stuck on the roof of her garage about two weeks ago, and the kids sometimes brought her mail from her mailbox to her front door so she wouldn't have to go and get it. She liked them, but she'd only known them for a month, not long enough to know who might want to hurt them, or what she was walking into.

Because she knew—without a shadow of a doubt—that she was going to go and find out what was going on.

She had to.

She couldn't do nothing if someone was in trouble.

She had to do whatever she could to help them.

It was a compulsion that had almost gotten her killed on more than one occasion, and it was the reason she was currently confined to a wheelchair.

As quickly and quietly as she could, Savannah started for the Fishers' house.

Four people lived there and she'd heard three gunshots; that meant someone hadn't been shot. Or one member of the family had just killed the others and might be about to commit suicide. She wished she'd had more than passing conversations about the weather and the neighborhood and the approaching festive season. If she knew a little about the family then she might be more prepared for what she was going to find.

Was one of them unstable?

Was it a home invasion?

Was there someone who was after the family?

Now that she thought about it, they never really talked about themselves. The kids were shy and polite, but they never said much. They parents *had* asked her a lot of questions about crime in the neighborhood, and Savannah had thought it was just because they were concerned about their family's safety, in general. But what if it was something else?

She was just coming through the front gate when she saw moving figures.

A man and a woman.

Was it Gavin and Violet?

But if it was, then where were the kids?

What was going on?

As the couple passed under a streetlight, it became apparent what was happening.

Savannah had never seen the man before, but the woman was definitely Violet. She was being held tightly against the man's chest; he had an arm hooked around her waist, and his other hand was pressed firmly over her mouth. He was half leading, half dragging her toward a car.

This was an abduction.

Someone had broken into the Fisher house, presumably shot Gavin and the kids and was kidnapping Violet.

It never even occurred to her not to try to do something.

"Hey!" she yelled out.

The man froze.

He turned to look at her, his face all shadows in the thin light.

Now that she was sitting here, face-to-face with a man who had more than likely just killed three people—including two children—she realized what a mistake this was.

What was she going to do to stop him?

He was huge, and she couldn't even walk.

She should have gone inside, called 911, and reported what she heard.

How had she thought this was a good idea?

Oh well, it was too late to back out now.

Screaming for help might be her best option. It was only eleven; some people might still be up, and even if they weren't, if she was loud enough, someone would surely wake up and hear her.

"Go back in your house and pretend you never saw this," the man growled at her.

He was giving her an out?

Did he not want to hurt her?

If she turned around, would he really let her live?

It was obvious Violet was who he really wanted.

But he didn't know her.

5

He didn't know that she couldn't walk away from someone who needed help no matter the cost to herself.

The only tool at her disposal right now was her voice. She couldn't fight him, and she doubted she could talk him out of it, but she could still get help. Maybe if she screamed, he might panic, leave Violet, and run.

Savannah was just opening her mouth to yell at the top of her lungs when there was a sudden blur of movement as the man rushed at her.

Then she was flung backward at full force.

There was no time for her to attempt to regain control of her wheelchair.

She was spinning out of control.

She slammed into the metal gatepost.

Her head connected with a sickening thud.

The world exploded into blinding pain and then dissolved into nothingness.

DECEMBER 21ST

"Why are we out so early?"

Chloe grinned at her husband. Fin was so cute when he was pouting. "You have to be at the hospital by seven for your shift; we would have been awake anyway," she reminded him.

"Yeah, awake, but we could have spent a little extra time in bed."

She laughed. Sex was always on Fin's mind. More so than ever since they had gotten back together last Christmas. It was funny how much had changed in one year.

Just twelve months, and yet the difference between her life then and now was like black and white.

Last year she had been bordering on hopeless. She'd felt alone and depressed and been too filled with pain to even consider being happy again. And now, she had everything she had ever wanted. She was married to the man she loved, and in only a month, she was going to be holding her son in her arms for the first time.

It was still a little surreal.

And Chloe couldn't deny that she was pretty terrified. Not at becoming a mother, but that something would happen and things would go wrong like they did last time.

Fin did his best to help assuage her fears, but to be honest, it didn't do any good because she knew that inside he was just as afraid as she was. There was no amount of cool, calm, and collected masks in the world that he could put on that would hide his fears from her. She felt them—every time he touched her, every time he spoke to her about the baby, every time they did something to prepare for bringing their son home with them.

They were both so scared that they would lose this son just like they'd lost their first son.

Chloe wished she could just snap her fingers and the birth would be over and her baby would be born safe and sound and home with them.

But she couldn't.

She just had to hope and pray that everything would go smoothly this time. Having Fin by her side helped. She didn't need him to be strong and try to convince them both that everything would be okay. She just needed him to be there.

She reached over and rested her hand on his thigh. He immediately removed one hand from the steering wheel and interlaced their fingers.

"You okay?" he asked, his blue eyes full of concern.

Chloe smiled. She really was okay, but she appreciated his concern. She was so glad they'd found a way to work past the pain, guilt, and anger and find their way back to each other.

"I'm fine. And you know we wouldn't have still been in bed if we were at home." She smiled. She didn't want to get dragged back down into that dark place. She had Fin and they were expecting a baby; she couldn't let her fears ruin this time in her life.

"I bet I could have persuaded you." Fin waggled his dark eyebrows at her and she couldn't help but laugh. He probably *could* have persuaded her to stay in bed if she hadn't already made plans with Savannah. "I still don't get why you need to be at her house so early."

"Why does it matter?" she asked. "You only left fifteen minutes earlier than you would have anyway." Chloe wasn't sure why she wanted to be at Savannah's house so early in the morning. Maybe because she was worried about her friend, and the more time she spent with her, the more chance she had of pulling Savannah out of the funk she'd been stuck in over the last twelve months.

"Savannah is lucky to have you." Fin lifted her hand and pressed a kiss to it.

"I don't know how to help her." She and Savannah had been best friends for a long time, and she would do anything to help her. But she couldn't. Nothing she tried had helped to lift Savannah's spirits, and it made her feel so helpless. Chloe would do whatever it took to help her friend, but she didn't know what to try next.

"You help her just by being there," Fin assured her. "But she needs to find her own way to rebuild her life."

"I want to help her."

"I know you do, and I love you for it, but she has to find her own way. All you can do is be there for her, support her, make sure that she knows you love her, and you do all of that."

Chloe remained unconvinced.

She'd feel better if she had made at least a little progress, but Savannah was just as lost and depressed as she had been this time last year.

"I'll walk you in," Fin announced as he parked the car across the street from Savannah's house.

"I can walk in myself." She shot him an amused smile; he'd become ridiculously overprotective since they'd found out she was pregnant. Especially since *he* had been released from prison early. They weren't supposed to talk about him. Fin didn't like to even mention his name—as though by saying it they could summon him. Her husband might want to pretend that Marcus King didn't exist, but she couldn't let it go. She was doing whatever she could to get him put back behind bars where he belonged

"Of course you can," he agreed. "I'm still walking you in."

As she climbed out of the car, Chloe tugged her reindeer beanie on and pulled the snowflake scarf Fin had given her for her last birthday tighter around her neck. While the weather had been cold, it hadn't been cold enough to snow, and she was missing the beautiful fluffy white covering over everything. She hoped it snowed before Christmas.

Fin took her hand as they crossed the street. Chloe loved holding hands; it always felt so intimate. Even when they were just sitting together on the couch in the evenings hanging out and watching TV, she would entwine their fingers.

Dawn was just bringing a tinge of light to the sky, and something caught her eye as they got closer to Savannah's front gate.

Her cop instincts started to tingle.

She may be on maternity leave but that didn't mean that she switched off her FBI agent instincts.

Something felt wrong.

"Fin, do you see that?"

"What?"

"There." She pointed at a dark puddle on the sidewalk.

"Is that blood?"

"I think so."

"Stay behind me." Fin tried to push her behind him, but Chloe just pushed past him. *She* was the FBI agent; *he* was the doctor.

She hurried the rest of the way to Savannah's gate ... where she found her friend lying, unmoving on the ground.

Her wheelchair was toppled over, lying on the ground beside her.

A blanket partially covered her, and her black cat was curled up at her side.

While she scanned the area, searching the dark yard for anything out of place, Fin ran to Savannah and dropped down at her side, his hand immediately moving to her neck. Chloe couldn't see anyone, but someone had obviously been here at some point. Savannah wouldn't have just fallen out of her wheelchair. What was she doing out here anyway? And how long had she been here?

"Fin?"

"She's alive," her husband answered crisply, in full-on doctor mode. One hand was skimming Savannah's body in search of injuries, while his other was holding her wrist taking her pulse.

"There's blood; how badly is she hurt?" Chloe heard her voice quiver. She wasn't new to crime scenes or victims or blood, but this was her best friend.

"It looks like she hit her head."

"How long has she been here?"

"Long enough to be hypothermic. We need to get her inside."

"Is it safe to move her?"

"I need to get her body temperature up." Fin looked worried, and that amped up her own fears.

"Is she going to die?" she asked, almost afraid to hear the answer.

"Call an ambulance," was Fin's only response, as he shrugged out of his coat and wrapped it around Savannah, then carefully picked her up.

Chloe yanked out her phone and called 911 as she followed Fin down the front path, scrambling around inside her bag for her keys. On her key chain, she had a set to Savannah's house.

"Grab blankets and a hot water bottle if you know she has one. And I need a first aid kit so I can bandage her wound." Fin barked out instructions.

With a look at Savannah's still form and deathly white skin, she hurried to collect what Fin asked for.

When she returned, she watched in anxious silence as Fin placed the hot water bottle on Savannah's chest then wrapped the blankets around her. Then he rummaged through the first aid kit, pulling out gauze, which he folded up and pressed to a bloody gash on her forehead.

As he was wrapping a bandage around her head, Savannah began to stir.

"Savannah?" Chloe leaned in close. She needed to know that her friend was okay, and she needed to know what had happened.

"Chloe?" Savannah's voice was the merest hint of a whisper.

"What happened?" she asked, ignoring Fin's frown. He was a doctor; his instincts were to heal. But she was an FBI agent; her instincts were to protect. And in order to do that, she needed to know what she was up against.

Savannah murmured something that sounded like violence.

"Violence?" she repeated. "Did someone hurt you?" A whole string of scenarios were running through her head, each one more horrific than the one before.

Savannah shook her head, and her eyes fluttered, half opened, then fell closed. "Violet."

"Violet?" Fin asked.

Savannah nodded.

"Who's Violet?"

"Her new next-door neighbor." How was the woman mixed up in whatever had happened? Perching on the side of the couch beside her friend, she asked, "Savannah, did someone hurt Violet? Did someone hurt you?"

"Gunshots. Man." Savannah's teeth were chattering, making it hard to understand what she was saying. That added to the fact that she was clearly weak, and Chloe knew she wasn't getting any more out of her.

"Stay with her," she ordered her husband.

"Where are you going?" Fin eyed her suspiciously.

"Violet's house." *Where else would she be going?*

"Chloe, you're pregnant."

She knew that. And she knew that she could be putting her baby in a dangerous situation, but there might be people who needed her.

Reading in her face that she intended to go anyway, her husband tried another approach. "You don't even have a weapon."

"But I know where Savannah keeps her gun." She was already heading to get it. Grabbing the key from the kitchen, she went to the hall closet and unlocked the box inside and pulled out the gun. "I love you." She gave Fin a quick kiss.

"Chloe," he said. She could see the terror in his eyes and feel it rolling off him.

"I'll be okay: I promise," she assured him.

She pressed a kiss to Savannah's icy cheek, then hurried outside.

With no idea what she was going to encounter, Chloe headed into the Fisher family's yard. The front door stood open, which did not bode well. She had no idea what had happened except that it had something to do with Violet Fisher, a man, and gunshots.

The house was quiet, and she made her way toward the bedrooms.

The first one she encountered was the master.

She only needed to take one step inside to know that there was nothing she could do.

Gavin Fisher was dead.

Violet Fisher was nowhere to be seen.

Continuing down the hall, she came to Heath Fisher's room.

Again, she was met with the helplessness that came with being unable to do anything.

There was only one family member left to find, and she didn't hold out much hope that she was going to find anything different in the last bedroom.

Crossing the hall, she opened the door.

Twelve-year-old Peta Fisher lay on the carpet in a huge puddle of blood and lifted her head.

* * * * *

8:27 A.M.

He had failed her.

He'd thought he'd done the right thing, but now he was second-guessing himself.

Maybe he should have put officers on her. Maybe he should have put her in protective custody. Maybe he should have told her to leave the country.

What it all boiled down to, he hadn't done the one thing he'd needed to, to ensure her safety.

He hadn't caught him in time.

And now Violet Fisher was missing, her husband and son dead, and her twelve-year-old daughter was fighting for her life in the hospital.

He'd really messed up.

FBI agent Jett Crane walked down the path to the front door of the house the Fisher family had moved into only a month ago. *He* was the one who had told her to move. He'd thought he was doing the right thing. He also thought it would give him enough time to find him before he found Violet.

Obviously, he'd been wrong.

And Violet and her family had paid the price.

He would do whatever it took to find her and bring her home alive. He was not going to fail her again. Whatever it took, he would do it. Whatever sacrifices he had to make, he would. Nothing was going to stop him from saving her. Nothing.

"Jett."

He turned when he heard his name and saw Tom Drake striding toward him. They had been friends years ago but drifted apart. He would have been glad to have the man work this case with him if it were any other case. But this case was personal. He was working this case alone. This case was his.

"What are you doing here?" he asked, probably harsher than he should have, but he didn't want to waste time having to explain this case to someone. He just wanted to end this.

"Working this case with you," Tom replied evenly.

"I'm not looking for a partner." Jett arched a challenging brow.

"It's not up to you. We can waste time and debate this, or you can just accept it and get me up to speed." Tom stood and patiently waited.

Jett sighed.

He didn't want to do this.

He wanted to tell Tom to leave.

He wanted to argue that this was his problem to solve.

But, most of all, he wanted to avoid a new partner at all costs.

Still, it didn't look like he had a choice.

Tom was here, and no doubt his superiors weren't going to be interested in listening to his arguments of why he should work this case alone.

Jett supposed that if he had to work with someone, it might as well be Tom Drake. At least he knew the man pretty well. He had known Tom back when the man had been married the first time, and he knew what had happened to rip him and his wife apart. He also knew that Tom and Hannah had reconciled and were now the proud parents to a five-month-old baby girl.

If he had to trust someone, Tom was a good choice.

"His name is Blake Sedenker, and he's obsessed with Violet Fisher," he told Tom.

"He wants her dead?"

"No. He wants *her.*"

"He's a stalker."

"A dangerous one. He knows the system. He knows what we're going to do and how to avoid us. He was starting to circle in closer, getting ready to abduct her. I told Violet to move. I thought it would give me enough time to find him."

"It's not your fault, Jett," Tom consoled.

But he didn't want to be consoled.

It *was* his fault, and debating the issue was a waste of time. Time they didn't have. All that mattered was finding Violet. Not him and his feelings. Not the mistakes he'd made. Dwelling on should-haves and could-haves wasn't productive, and he didn't have time for anything that wasn't productive right now. There would be plenty of time to dwell on his mistakes later—once Violet was back home and with her daughter.

He turned abruptly and headed inside. He didn't want to be rude to Tom, but he just needed to keep moving. He needed to find Violet, and the longer it took, the colder the trail grew.

He didn't need to look at the front door to know the lock had been picked. It was how Blake always entered Violet's home. He would have used a pair of bolt cutters to cut the chain, then he would have disabled the security system. It didn't matter how many times Violet reset it and how creative she got with inventing the code, Blake always seemed to be able to crack it.

Jett didn't bother searching the rest of the house. Blake was always direct. He would have gone straight to the bedrooms. He wasn't interested in anything but Violet. He knew that wasting time was risky and that the more contact he had with the things in the house, the bigger the chances that he would leave behind evidence that would lead them to him.

Sometimes knowing who you were looking for didn't make it any easier to find them.

He knew Blake Sedenker was the man he was chasing, but every time he thought he had pinned down where he was hiding out, he found he was either wrong, or Blake had already moved on.

This game of cat-and-mouse had been going on for almost a year now.

He bypassed the master bedroom and headed straight for the kids' rooms.

"You don't want to do the parents' room first?" Tom asked.

"He started back here."

"How do you know?"

"I know him. He did the children first."

"Wouldn't he want to eliminate the biggest threat first? That would have been the husband."

"He didn't see any of them as a threat," he answered simply. "He would have wanted to do the kids before he went into Violet's room because he wouldn't want to risk her pulling a weapon on him after he killed her husband. If he left her for last, he could kill the husband, then grab Violet and run without having to backtrack through the house to take out the children."

"Why kill the family at all? If he wants Violet, he could have taken her and left them alive." Protective anger filled Tom's brown eyes, and Jett knew he was thinking about the possibility of anyone hurting his wife and daughter and what he would do to that person.

"He doesn't want any ties to her past. He wants to be the only one in her life," Jett explained as he opened the door to Heath Fisher's room. It was a room typical of an almost-teenage boy: messy, sports paraphernalia everywhere, and pictures of who was obviously his celebrity crush. Heath was a typical kid, and he had held up remarkably well with everything he had had to endure with his mother's stalker.

Nothing in the room looked out of place.

Except for the spray of blood on the headboard and the blood-soaked mattress.

Heath's body still lay on the bed.

A single bullet hole in his forehead.

The kill had been clean and quick, and Heath would never have seen it coming.

"He would have used a silencer," he said almost absently. This boy had had such a bright future, and it had been ripped away from him. Heath would never get to live out his dreams, and there was only one person to blame for that.

Actually, there were two.

Blake Sedenker and himself.

Jett knew that realistically, there wasn't anything more he could have done. He'd offered protective custody, and Violet had declined. He could have pushed harder. He could have put someone on her. But that probably would have tipped Blake off, and even in protective custody, she probably wouldn't have been safe from a man who had too much insider knowledge.

Before he could wallow, he turned and headed for the room across the hall.

Peta's room.

The girl was his first mistake.

Somehow, she had survived.

He'd shot her in the head, but somehow, the bullet hadn't killed her.

Yet.

She was currently undergoing emergency surgery, but for now, she was alive.

From the blood trail on the carpet, it looked like she had managed to drag herself out of bed and tried to get to the door to get help. She hadn't made it all the way, but the girl was a fighter, and he had to believe that she would pull through. When he brought Violet home, he didn't want her to come back to nothing.

"Heath first, then Peta, then Gavin," Tom said. "Why that order?"

"Heath was born first."

"That matters to him?"

"Blake likes order. He needs it; he seeks it out."

"Gavin was killed like Heath, a bullet straight to the head. He wasn't interested in them suffering; he just wanted them eliminated."

"Blake has never shown any animosity toward Violet's family. They were just in the way. Not killing Peta was his first mistake, but he made another. He got sloppy because he decided he couldn't wait any longer to get his hands on Violet. He left a witness behind."

Apparently, someone had stumbled upon the abduction and

lived to tell about it.

It wasn't like Blake to leave a witness alive. What was it about this particular woman that had caused him to spare her?

This neighbor woman must have heard the shots and gone to investigate. Why? What kind of person ran straight toward trouble instead of doing the sensible thing and dialing 911?

"What do you know about this woman?" Jett couldn't help but be suspicious of anyone who was involved in this case. Somehow, Blake had managed to find Violet. Had this woman been the one to tip him off? He couldn't think of another reason why she was still alive.

"Jett, you know it's Savannah, right?"

Savannah?

His Savannah?

Everything, but driving to the hospital to see her and make sure she was actually still alive, fled from his mind.

* * * * *

9:09 A.M.

Her hands ached, and her knuckles were bleeding. She couldn't see it, but Violet could feel the blood coating her bruised joints.

She didn't stop, though.

She curled her hands into fists and hammered on the walls. There had to be a way out. Common sense told her that there wasn't, but she had thrown common sense to the wind along with her mind.

Right now, it was a pure animal fight or flight instinct that fueled her.

Survival.

That was all she cared about.

Violet uncurled her hands and began to claw at the walls. If she couldn't pound her way out, maybe she could scratch her way out.

She knew that was ridiculous. The walls of wherever he had stashed her were obviously not going to break down because she hit them. If they would, he never would have put her in here.

He was never letting her go.

She knew that.

As much as she was trying to fight it, block it out, pretend that it wasn't there, fear was creeping through her body. It had snuck in like a thief in the night. It came in when she wasn't ready for it, and now it was growing inside her. Filling her up. Infiltrating every cell of her body.

It was going to kill her.

Maybe that was a good thing.

Maybe, by the time he came back for her, she'd already be dead.

At least then, she would be spared whatever horrific things Blake intended to do to her.

What was worse was that she knew *exactly* what he intended to do to her because he'd told her.

He'd been stalking her for over a year now.

He'd been very clear that he wanted her, and nothing was going to stop him from getting her.

If Violet had known what he was going to do to get her, she would have agreed to go with him willingly. If it meant keeping her family alive, she would've gladly sacrificed herself.

But now it was too late for that.

It was too late for everything.

They were dead, and she was here.

She wasn't under any illusions. She was never going to escape from him. Blake was smart and strong and meticulous. He would have planned out every single detail, gone over every single problem that might arise or what might go wrong and worked out contingencies.

This was her life now.

He had gotten what he wanted. She was his prisoner—his

property—to do with whatever he pleased.

Agent Crane wouldn't stop looking for her. Ever. But even if he found her, what did she have to go back to?

Nothing.

Blake had killed them all.

Her husband.

Her son.

Her daughter.

All of them were gone.

Without them, she had nothing to live for.

Giving up her desperate attempts at escape, Violet sank to the floor. Her wrists were still bound together with a plastic zip tie. Its sharp edges had cut through the skin on her wrists, but she didn't care. She didn't feel any pain. She was numb now.

It'd only been a few hours since Blake had broken into her house, shot her family, and kidnapped her, but she had already ridden a roller coaster of emotions: shock, disbelief, denial, acceptance. Now she had settled into an empty zone of nothingness.

The space she was in was tiny, not enough room for her to stretch her legs out, but even if she could have, she wouldn't. She wanted to curl herself up into as small a ball as possible—as though that could help her to disappear.

Right now, that was what she wanted.

To disappear.

Death, but death with no pain.

For over a year, she had been fighting to keep control of her life as Blake Sedenker was determined to make it spin out of control. She fought to not feel like a victim. She fought to make people take her stalking case seriously. She fought to keep her marriage together as the stresses of being stalked weighed down on their relationship. She fought to shield and protect her kids as best as she could from all that was going on around them. She had fought to feel safe.

Well, she was done fighting.

Enough was enough.

It didn't matter now anyway.

Nothing mattered.

With her knees up against her chest, she buried her face in her arms and let her tears flow. She didn't sob; she was too exhausted for that, so she just cried quietly.

Violet didn't know how long she sat there weeping, but the next thing she knew, the light was spilling into the dark space, and hands were wrapping around her biceps.

Blake crouched in front of her and hooked a finger under her chin to force her head up. Through her teary eyes, she could see that he was looking at her anxiously. "Sweetheart, what's wrong? Why are you crying?" One hand cupped her cheek, and with his other, he caught her tears with his fingertips.

What a joke. He slaughtered her family, abducted her, and locked her in this horrible little room. How did he expect her to act?

Did he think she would be happy?

Did he think that now that she was here with him, she was going to fall in love with him?

Did he think she would be pleased that he had killed her family in cold blood?

Ever since he had thrown her in the back of his car, she'd been waiting for her opportunity to strike. She didn't care that it was pointless. She didn't care that it would make him angry. She had nothing to lose, and she wanted nothing more than to take out all her pent-up hostility over everything he'd put her through the last year squarely on him.

With a shriek, she flung herself at him.

It didn't matter that her hands were tied together. She just swung them at him, connecting firmly with his cheekbone, making a very satisfying thud.

Spurred on by this small victory, she scratched at him with her ragged nails. Violet knew she wasn't going to cause him any real damage. She just wanted to inflict as much pain as she could before he stopped her.

Lines of red marred his face.

Bright red blood.

It sent a rush of endorphins through her system, giving her a high unlike anything else she had ever experienced.

She had done that.

She'd made him bleed, and it wasn't enough.

Bloodlust.

She had never experienced it before, but no one else had ever done to her the things Blake Sedenker had.

She wanted to rip him to shreds, piece by piece, enjoying every drop of blood that was shed and every single scream she tore from his lips.

Before she could make her dreams come true, she was dragged off the floor and thrown across the room. Her body bounced off the wall and landed on the floor with a thud.

Pain coursed through her, but Violet had entered a place where pain no longer existed. All that existed was her anger.

She staggered to her feet and launched herself at Blake again.

He was ready for her this time and snapped an arm around her chest, pinning her with her arms at her side. He was so much bigger than her. Even though she wiggled and squirmed, she couldn't budge his arm even an inch. It was like being held down by a tree trunk.

One of his large hands moved to her face, covering her mouth and her nose and cutting off her air supply.

"I don't want to hurt you, sweetheart, but that behavior is unacceptable in this house," he drawled in her ear. She hated it when he called her that. It implied intimacy, and there was nothing she wanted less than that developing between her and her captor.

Violet had no intention of developing Stockholm Syndrome.

What she felt for Blake would never change.

She hated him with an all-consuming passion.

Her fingers and toes began to tingle as lack of oxygen cut off blood supply to her extremities. Her pulse began to rush in her ears like wind. Black dots began to dance about in front of her eyes.

She didn't fight it.

What was the point?

Her only other option was spending the rest of her life as Blake Sedenker's prisoner, praying that Agent Crane found her. It was a long shot. He had been hunting Blake for over a year without success. Why should that change now? If by some fluke he did manage to find her, she would go home to nothing.

Or she could die a quick death now.

She knew what she'd prefer.

Violet let herself float away.

Just as she was reaching the shores of blissful unconsciousness, she was yanked back when Blake removed his hand, and her lungs reflexively dragged in a long, harsh breath.

Tears leaked from the corners of her eyes.

Even death had deserted her.

She was truly and utterly alone.

* * * * *

10:16 A.M.

Savannah wasn't sure if she wanted to throw up, jump into a bath full of boiling hot water to warm her bone-chilled body, or go back to sleep for about a month.

Or maybe a mixture of all three.

She probably would have gone back to sleep, but someone was yelling.

No … more than one person.

It sounded like an argument.

Now that she thought about it, she believed the argument must have been going on for a while because it had infiltrated her dreams.

As horrible as she felt, she mustn't be in too bad a shape because she remembered with horrifying clarity, everything that had happened the night before. At least, she assumed it was only the night before, but she wasn't really sure how much time had passed.

The more she thought, the more awake she became, sleep drifting away. She may as well open her eyes, get some answers. She was pretty sure that she had told Fin and Chloe about Violet and the gunshots.

She didn't remember anything after being knocked backward and hitting her head, but she must have passed out and spent the night outside. Chloe had been going to come and spend the day, so she and her husband must have found her. Fin was a doctor and had probably treated her. Whatever he'd done had been enough to bring her around, and she had told them what had happened. She doubted it was soon enough to help Violet, but at least her family wasn't lying dead in their home.

Savannah tentatively opened her eyes. The room was dully lit, and the blinds were closed, but she could see the light peeking around the edges. An IV ran into the back of her hand, and she was tightly wrapped in warmed blankets. Chloe sat in a chair beside her bed.

Although she wanted nothing more than to burrow into her little cocoon of warmth and hibernate for the winter, she angled her body in Chloe's direction.

Her head retaliated the small movement by sending arrows of pain shooting back and forth inside her skull. The rest of her body also protested with a symphony of duller aches and pains. She bit back the bile that threatened to choke her and breathed through the pain. Something she, unfortunately, had a lot of experience doing.

"Savannah?" Chloe stood and leaned over the bed's guardrail. "Are you all right?"

As all right as she could be considering she was once again back in the hospital. "I'm all right," she assured her friend. She and Chloe had been friends for a long time; they had dreamed about going through the FBI academy together, graduating together, having their dream job together.

But life didn't always give you what you wanted.

A lesson she had had to learn several times over.

She loved her job as a crime scene technician, but some days she still wished that she had never been attacked. Or that the damage to her hip had been less severe and she hadn't been left with a permanent limp.

Now she didn't even have her forensics job.

Thanks to a second attack on the same hip a year ago, she was now confined to a wheelchair. Her doctors had told her that if she put in the work at physical therapy, then she should be able to walk again, but she was afraid to try.

What if they were wrong?

What if she tried her best and failed?

She couldn't take that risk.

It would destroy her to get her hopes up only to have them dashed. She'd already lost so much because of that one night— she couldn't lose anything else. She might not like being confined to a wheelchair, but at least it was safe. She knew what to expect, she had adjusted, she had accepted things for what they were. It was what it was, wishing couldn't change things, and physical therapy might not either. So, she wasn't doing it.

Part of her wanted to.

Well, really, most of her wanted to.

So many times in the last twelve months, she had picked up her phone, intending to call her physical therapist and book an appointment, but every time she did, a paralyzing fear gripped her.

What if she wasn't strong enough to get better? And even if it worked and she could walk again, what else was she going to lose?

Savannah couldn't believe that she wouldn't lose something else.

The first time, she had worked night and day to walk again, and, in the end, she hadn't just lost her dream job but the man of her dreams too.

Now she may not have a guy in her life, but she was sure she'd lose something.

She just couldn't risk it.

No matter how much she wanted to, she was just too afraid.

"Where did you just go?"

She blinked and found that Chloe had perched on the edge of her bed.

"Just thinking," she answered vaguely, Savannah didn't want to explain to anyone how afraid she was about trying to walk again. "When can I go home?" She wanted out of this bed and out of this building. Right now. The sooner, the better. Immediately, if possible. She had spent last Christmas in the hospital, and she didn't want to do that again.

"You're hypothermic, and you have a concussion," Chloe said. "You're lucky to be alive. You were out in the cold all night. If you hadn't had that blanket with you, and it hadn't landed on you, and that cat of yours hadn't spent the night curled up against you, then you probably would have been dead by the time Fin and I found you."

"Sequin slept beside me? She was the reason I was out there anyway." She chanced moving again and carefully dragged herself into a semi-sitting position. Her head spun like a carousel, taking her stomach along with it, and she very nearly gave up and sank back down, abandoning herself to unconsciousness.

"Take it easy, it's too soon to be trying to move so much." Chloe's hands held her shoulders and gently pressed her back to lie against the pillows.

Savannah fought against her. "Not too soon if I want to go home."

"Savan—"

"What do you know about Violet and her family?" she interrupted. She didn't want to be coddled; she wanted answers, and then she wanted to go home.

"Gavin and Heath were killed instantly," Chloe said gently, taking her hands and squeezing supportively.

She had been expecting to hear that, and yet she still felt the blow of her friend's words. It wasn't that she had been close with the family, but no one deserved to be killed like that, certainly not a lovely father and his twelve-year-old son.

Her brow furrowed.

Chloe had said that Gavin and Heath had been killed, and she knew Violet had been abducted, but what about Peta?

"She's alive," Chloe obviously read the question in her face. "Barely, but she's still holding on. Last I heard she was in recovery."

Relief flooded through her, washing away some of the pain and nausea. "Peta is alive. That's a miracle."

"As much as you still being alive." Chloe brushed at a stray tear that escaped. "I could have lost you."

Savannah tightened her grip on her best friend's hands. "But you didn't. I'm fine. I mean, I feel like garbage, but I'll live." How she managed to keep surviving these life-threatening situations she was thrown into, she had no idea.

"Why don't you close your eyes and try to get some sleep," Chloe suggested. "I know you want to go home, but I think Fin was saying that they still need to get your body temperature up a bit first."

Now she was too wired to sleep.

Her mind kept replaying last night's events, trying to see something she had missed that could be the key to finding Violet.

Where was she?

Who had taken her?

What were they doing to her?

She had messed up last night by not going straight to her phone and calling for help, and because of that, Violet may lose her life.

"Is a cop coming by to take my statement?" she asked. She wasn't sure she could give them much, but she'd try to remember any little detail that might be helpful.

"Uh, yes," Chloe said, but she looked weird.

Too tired to figure out why, she asked, "I heard arguing outside, what's going on?"

"It's nothing." Chloe shot her a bright smile.

Too bright.

Something was going on.

"Don't try to protect me. I have a bump on my head; I'm not a child. Who was arguing?"

Chloe's gaze darted nervously about. "It was just Fin, and, well, actually, Fin and the cop who's working this case. Well, not a cop exactly, an FBI agent."

She narrowed her eyes in suspicion and was rewarded with a sharp stab of pain in her head. "Why is Fin arguing with the FBI agent working Violet's case? I know he's a doctor and he's probably worried about my medical condition, but I'm fine. Go and tell your husband to send in the agent so I can just get this over with."

"Savannah," Chloe said gently, "the agent is Jett."

* * * * *

10:51 A.M.

"You can't keep me from seeing her indefinitely," Jett growled. He had been trying to get into Savannah's hospital room for the last few hours, but so far, Fin Patrick hadn't budged.

Jett knew Fin. He had been Chloe's boyfriend, and he'd heard that Fin and Chloe had broken up, but last year they had reconciled and were now married and expecting a baby.

He kept close tabs on the people in Savannah's life.

He kept close tabs on Savannah's life.

Although, apparently, not close enough.

He hadn't known her address. It had been a deliberate decision. He didn't want to know where she lived because if he did, the temptation to turn up there and force her to forgive him and take him back would be overwhelming.

But that wasn't what she wanted.

She had ended things between them, and he had respected that. Well, stalking aside. He just hadn't been able to make a clean break. He couldn't just let her walk out of his life. He still loved her, and he'd always wanted her back. He hadn't dated anyone in the almost three years since they'd broken up. He hadn't wanted to. No woman could come close to Savannah.

If he had known that Savannah was the neighbor who had witnessed Blake kidnapping Violet and been injured in the process, he would have skipped going to the Fisher house and come straight to the hospital. He should have known. Who else would go running straight toward danger instead of running away from it like a normal person?

She couldn't help herself.

It didn't matter how many times she was hurt in the process— if someone was in need, she would do whatever she could to help them.

Now, Savannah needed him.

Because of her need to try to save people, she had gotten herself on Blake Sedenker's radar. Jett couldn't guarantee that he wouldn't come after her. This case had taken on a whole new level of urgency, and instead of working on solving it, he was stuck out here in the hall because the doctor wouldn't let him in to see Savannah.

Enough was enough—he wasn't waiting another second.

"Get out of the way, Fin."

"She needs to rest," Fin said in that overly patient voice that doctors used. It was infuriating.

"She's had time to rest."

"She could have died. She was out there all night, and besides the hypothermia, she has a nasty head wound."

Jett didn't need to be reminded that she was injured. He hadn't been able to think of anything else since he learned that Savannah was the injured neighbor. It was driving him insane that he hadn't been able to see her yet. He needed to convince himself that she really was alive and relatively in one piece.

"I. Need. To. See. Her. Now." He over-enunciated each word. He didn't want to have to play the FBI card, but he would if Fin gave him no choice. Savannah was the only witness in a federal case; there was nothing preventing him from walking in there and interviewing her. He was only playing nice because he wanted to make sure that Savannah was really and truly okay.

"Jett," Fin said gently, shedding the clinical doctor persona to instead sound like a concerned friend. "She won't want to see you."

He knew that.

He wasn't walking into this blind.

He knew that Savannah was still angry and hurt about the choices he'd made three years ago. But regardless of whether she liked it or not, she was stuck with him for the time being. She was a witness in his case, and she was now potentially in the sights of a dangerous man—he wasn't going anywhere.

"I appreciate that you're looking out for her," he told Fin, deliberately calming himself. Going into Savannah's room as emotional and worked up as he was right now wasn't going to help. "But I don't care. She'll have to deal with it. I've given her time. Three years' worth of time. Now I'm back, and I'm not going anywhere."

Well, that wasn't entirely true.

If he walked in there and he read in her face that she no longer loved him, then he would protect her, work this case, and then walk away.

But if she still loved him, then all bets were off. This time he wouldn't quietly go away. This time he would fight for her until he won her back.

With a sigh, Fin stepped away from the door.

Like a wild animal that had finally been set free, Jett threw open the door and stepped inside.

Savannah's head immediately snapped in his direction, and she winced at the sudden movement. A square white bandage was taped to her forehead, and she was swaddled in so many blankets, all that was visible of her was her pale face.

Despite all of that, she was the singular most beautiful thing he'd ever seen.

Her delicate features, her long blonde hair that fanned out around her on the pillow, those huge blue eyes framed by impossibly long lashes.

She was breathtaking.

Three years hadn't changed a thing. She was every bit as beautiful as she'd been back then.

If he wanted her back—and he did—then he was going to have to play this right. He knew he'd hurt her badly when he hadn't been there for her when she needed him, and as much as he hated knowing that he had caused her pain, he knew that, at the time, he had made the right choice. What Jett had been doing instead of being there for Savannah had been unavoidable. He'd tried to explain it to her, but she hadn't wanted to listen.

This time around, she would listen to his explanation.

"Hi, Savannah," he said, sounding every bit as lovestruck as he felt.

"Jett," she nodded briskly, wincing again.

He searched her gaze, looking for signs that she still cared about him. If she hadn't been injured, then she would probably have been able to muster a better poker face. As it was, he could read every single emotion flying around inside her. Anger, pain, longing, loss, fear, a little bit of lust, and, most importantly, love.

He let out a breath he hadn't even realized he was holding.

Savannah still loved him; everything else they could work out.

"You know I'm working Violet's case." He drew a chair up to her bedside.

"Chloe told me." She nodded, wincing again.

"Stop moving your head; it's hurting you," he reprimanded tenderly, clutching his hands in his lap to keep from brushing his knuckles across her cheek. They weren't a couple—yet—so he couldn't touch her or hold her or kiss her, even if there was nothing more he'd rather do than crush his mouth to hers.

She ignored him. "How's Violet's daughter doing?"

It was just like her to be more worried about everyone else rather than herself. "She's doing well—stable. I have to ask you some questions about last night. Is that okay?" As much as he wanted a reconciliation with Savannah, he couldn't forget his responsibilities to Violet Fisher.

This time, she didn't nod. "Yes. Ask whatever you need. I'm not sure how much I can give you, but I'll do my best."

He had no doubt about that. "Can you tell me exactly what you saw and heard last night?"

She drew in a deep breath, then began. "I was taking Sequin outside to go to the bathroom before we went to bed. It was late, and I was cold, but she disappeared."

Jett remembered the cat; it was gorgeous with silky black fur dotted with small gold spots that looked like sequins.

"I was about to give up on her when I heard something that sounded like a muffled gunshot."

Just as he'd thought, Blake had used a suppressor.

"At first, I thought I had imagined it, so I was going to go inside, but then I heard it again. I was going toward the Fisher house, but just as I was going through my gate, I saw Violet with a man."

Instead of focusing on the fact that she had stupidly put herself in danger, he asked, "Did you get a good look at the man?"

"Not really … it was dark. He was tall, though … really tall, and he was dragging Violet toward a car. I yelled at him and he stopped and I realized that maybe I had made a mistake."

A small hint of pink tinted her cheeks as she realized the gravity of the mistake she had made. She was lucky to be alive, and not just because she survived the hypothermia. Blake could have killed her. He *should* have killed her. It wasn't like him to have left her alive.

"He told me to go home and forget I ever saw anything," she continued. "I knew the only chance I had at stopping him was screaming. I was just opening my mouth to when he shoved me. I remember being thrown backward and then pain in my head. After that, it's all a blank until I woke up in my living room with Chloe and Fin at my side."

Jett was struggling to keep it together.

He really could have lost her.

She had come closer than she realized to losing her life.

"Was the car he was dragging Violet to a black van?"

Her blue eyes sharpened. "You know who took her."

"I do. Was it?"

"Yes, I think so. Who is it? Who killed Violet's family and kidnapped her?"

"It was Blake Sedenker."

She gasped as recognition hit. "Blake?"

"Yes. He's been stalking Violet for the last year."

Sympathy filled her eyes, wiping away the lingering anger and resentment. "I'm sorry, Jett."

Her words filled him with hope. She knew him well enough to know without being told that he would be blaming himself for Violet's abduction. And despite the hurt he'd caused her, she still cared about him. Their love may be damaged, but it wasn't altogether gone.

"Can I have a moment alone with Savannah?" he asked Chloe and Fin, who had followed him into the room earlier.

"If she wants to go home later today, she really should get some more rest," Fin replied.

"I won't stay long," he promised.

"Savannah?" Chloe asked. She'd been giving him the evil eye the entire time and clearly wasn't enthused about the idea of leaving him alone with her friend. Jett was glad Savannah had such loyal people in her life.

"It's fine," Savannah said with so much calm detachment that she almost convinced him she felt nothing for him.

"I'll be right outside." Chloe kissed Savannah's cheek, gave him one last glare, then headed for the door.

"Five minutes," Fin cautioned as he and Chloe left.

Alone with Savannah for the first time in years, he just stared at her. If she hadn't been hurt, he would've been tempted to shove her up against the wall and kiss her until they forgot their own names.

"What do you want, Jett?" she asked tiredly.

"You," he replied simply.

"You can't have me."

"Do you still love me?"

She looked thrown by the question, unsure how best to answer.

"Do you?" he prodded, determined to make her admit it out loud.

"It's over between us."

"That's not what I asked."

"Jett," she pleaded, but he wasn't going to show her any mercy. He wanted an answer.

"Do you still love me, Savannah?"

She hesitated, but finally, she softly replied, "Yes."

That was all he needed to hear. "I'm not going anywhere. I won't be walking away again. I want you back," he informed her. Then before she had a chance to object, he stood, stooped over the bed, and pressed a kiss to her lips. Not the ravishing kind he wanted, but a gentle one in deference to her present injured condition.

Then, leaving Savannah staring after him, he left.

* * * * *

2:24 P.M.

"Tell me about your ex-partner. How did things get to this?" Tom asked.

This was exactly why he hadn't wanted a new partner.

Now he had to explain what had happened to Blake to turn him from a respected FBI agent to stalker and killer. Now, he had to explain how it was that he hadn't noticed the signs until it was too late.

He was the one person who should have seen it coming.

But he hadn't.

And Violet and her family had paid the price.

"Jett, you know what happened isn't—"

"Blake and I had been partners since I graduated." He interrupted Tom, unwilling to have anyone placate him. He knew he should have seen that Blake was devolving, and he hadn't. Therefore, he was just as much to blame for everything that had happened to the Fisher family as Blake himself.

"Longer than you've known Savannah," Tom said unnecessarily.

"Everything was fine up until about a year ago."

"What happened a year ago?"

"A case." One he didn't want to talk about.

"Jett." Tom sounded exasperated. "I know you want to work

this case on your own. I understand why. I get that because Blake was your partner, you think it's partially your fault. I'd tell you that it's not, but I get you won't believe it and don't want to hear it. But you have to accept that we are working this case together. I can't help if I don't know Blake's history and what led him to this place."

He sighed inwardly.

Mainly because he knew Tom was right.

He might not want to work this case with someone, but he had to.

"It was a mother who was selling her kids. She had four little daughters. The oldest was ten, the youngest was only two."

"Two?" Tom looked horrified.

"Two," Jett repeated.

It made him feel physically ill recounting this case. It had been by far the worst he had ever worked. He still remembered interviewing those little girls. The ten-year-old had had the deadest eyes he had ever seen on a person. She had recounted everything with a dull voice, and it had taken everything he had to remain composed throughout the interview. The eight-year-old had refused to speak. She'd been so afraid and so withdrawn that she wouldn't even come into the room as long as he was in it. The five-year-old had done nothing but cry, and the two-year-old had been too young to understand the horrors of what she had lived through.

Over the last year, he had been keeping tabs on those girls. They'd all been immediately placed with specialized foster carers who worked specifically with children who had been removed from the home due to some form of abuse. The girls were all undergoing counseling, and he prayed that with time, help, and support, one day, they might be able to live normal lives.

"The mother started using the kids' friends from school. When they came for play dates or sleepovers, she would take them along with her kids. One of those friends told an older sister what was going on, and thankfully, the older sister went straight to their parents, who went straight to the cops. Before we could get the girls, their mother fled with them. She was going to sell them on the black market so she'd have enough money to leave the country. Thankfully, we found the girls before they disappeared forever."

Two of the children had already been sold by the time they tracked her down. If they had been just twenty-four hours slower locating where she was hiding out with her kids, then those two youngest children would have been spirited out of the country and never heard from again.

"Dead or prison?" Tom asked.

Those were the only two options for someone who would sell her own children to pedophiles. "Dead. When we came for her, she committed suicide. She tried to take the children out with her, but thankfully, we were able to save them before they were hurt."

She had dragged all four kids to the top of the eleven-story apartment building where she had been living and threatened to throw the kids off if they didn't let her go. The oldest daughter had managed to grab the baby and escape, leaving two of the children still with her. She had actually thrown the five-year-old, and if it hadn't been for a firefighter on a ladder who had managed to snag ahold of the child's jacket and pull her to safety, the little girl would have died.

Jett was glad the woman had jumped.

People like that didn't deserve to live.

But the woman had set into motion a chain of events that had led them to where they were right now.

"What happened to Blake after the case?" Tom asked.

"At first, it seemed like he was doing okay. That case ... it was rough on all of us." He had wanted so badly to go and see Savannah during that time. He'd needed her. He had seriously considered doing it, but then she'd been hurt and spent a couple of weeks in the hospital. By that time, things with Blake had already started to spiral out of control.

"What were the first signs that he was struggling?"

"He had been drinking more, but it seemed like he was still handling things. I thought it was just a coping mechanism. That he'd get through it and move on. But then he started staying out all night and then coming to work drunk. There started to be problems in the home. He'd come home drunk at all hours of the night. He was scaring his daughter. Laila was eight, the same age as one of the Hobbs girls. That got to him more than anything else. He kept seeing his daughter as a victim. He turned up at her school a couple of times, drunk because he was convinced someone was going to hurt her."

"How does Violet Fisher play into all of this?"

"Violet was Laila's third-grade teacher. Laila started having problems at school. She became withdrawn, started failing subjects that she'd been getting straight As in before; she started having fights with her friends. Violet did everything she could to help Laila and Blake. But it was too late. About four months after the case, his wife kicked him out. She filed for divorce and sole custody of Laila. Blake showed up for the custody hearing drunk and lost his parental rights. Georgette started a new relationship, which she had to end when Blake started threatening the man. She tried to start over, and that was when the obsession with Violet really began."

Even after the divorce went through and he lost custody of his daughter, Jett hadn't realized just how bad things had gotten with Blake. He had still stupidly believed that his partner would pull it together. That he just needed some time. But time didn't always help.

"He started to show up at the school—always drunk. Then he'd show up at Violet's house. She got a restraining order, but he didn't care. He lost his job, he had no place to live, and he was sleeping in his car. He was sending Violet flowers and gifts, and he wouldn't stop going to the school and her house. Then one afternoon, he ran her car off the road and tried to abduct her. When several people stopped to help, he fled, but he wouldn't stay away. He was relentless. Every day, it was something new. I put cops on Violet's house, but it didn't do any good; he'd create a diversion and try to get to her. She had to quit her job because she couldn't leave the house."

Jett still wasn't sure what he could have done differently to end this game of cat-and-mouse he and his partner had been playing for the last eight months.

There had to have been something.

Something he could have said to Blake to stop him from slipping so far out of control, but his ex-partner had long since stopped listening to him.

"Blake knows you're the one looking for him?" Tom asked.

"He knows. He'll call me occasionally to threaten me to stay out of his business."

"Has he followed through on any of those threats?" Protectiveness shone from Tom's eyes like a guard dog.

"He's tried a few times, but he hasn't been successful. You should be careful and keep an eye on Hannah and Noelle. Once he finds out you're on this case now, there's a chance that he might go after you or your family." Jett waited to see if knowing there was a possibility that he and his family could be in danger would make Tom want off the case. He didn't think it would, but with Tom now being a father, his priorities weren't just his job anymore.

"Then we better find him before he hurts anyone else," Tom said determinedly.

Jett couldn't agree more.

* * * * *

4:39 P.M.

Everything felt so surreal.

Violet couldn't believe this was actually happening.

If only she could go back in time, she would never have tried to get in the middle of things and help Laila and her family.

No, she sighed to herself.

Even if she had known twelve months ago that things were going to spiral out of control and wind up like this, she still would have tried to help Laila. She couldn't stand back and not help a child in need. And Laila was such a sweet little girl. Violet had no idea that Blake was so unbalanced. She'd met him a couple of times at parent-teacher conferences, and when he'd picked Laila up from school, he'd seemed nice and normal—nothing like the psychopath he had turned out to be.

Maybe if she'd seen the signs, she wouldn't be here.

Here.

She was tied to a bed with ripped up strips of the sheet. He hadn't used chains, rope, or anything stereotypical "kidnap-ish." It was like he hadn't foreseen that she would try to attack him—like the idea that she wouldn't be happy with him had never occurred to him.

He had honestly believed that this was what she wanted.

He thought that if he could just get her away from her family that she would reciprocate his feelings.

He was delusional.

She didn't stand a chance of getting out of this. How could you reason with a crazy person? How do you escape from someone more than twice your size?

You didn't.

She squirmed on the bed, trying to find a comfortable position. He had left her tied up here for hours, ever since she'd tried to attack him. Her muscles were sore and stiff from being thrown against the wall and then being left in the same place for hours on end.

She didn't just ache; she felt filthy and disgusting. Although she had tried to hold on for as long as she could, eventually, the pain in her bladder had become too great, and she hadn't been able to hold it in any longer. Urinating all over herself for the first time since she was a toddler had been so humiliating. When her bowels had opened up behind her bladder, her mortification was complete.

Now she had to lie here in her own filth—dirty and smelly—and almost wishing Blake would return from whatever he was doing so she could beg him to please let her take a shower. She'd even promise not to run and not to try anything stupid, anything so long as she could just get clean.

What was going to happen to her if she spent weeks or months or even years with Blake? What if he kept her tied up like this indefinitely? What if he didn't let her shower? What if he didn't feed her or even give her water to drink?

Would he be able to break her down? Brainwash her until she would do whatever it took to get the basic necessities? That was how you brainwashed someone, right? You took everything away from them and then made them dependent on you. She had never thought she would be someone who would give in to their captor, but now she wasn't so sure. If Blake walked through that door right now, Violet honestly didn't know what she wouldn't use to bargain with if he would only let her take a shower.

She tried her best not to think about her current predicament, but there wasn't much else to think about. She could lie here and think about being covered in urine and feces, or she could think about her family.

Had they suffered?

Had they known what was happening?

Had they died instantly?

Violet didn't know the answers to any of those questions, and it killed her.

She had been awakened by the muffled sound of the gunshot, and when her eyes popped open, she had seen her husband's lifeless body lying beside her. She had known he was dead because his eyes had been open and staring sightlessly at the ceiling. She didn't think that he'd suffered. She hadn't heard anything else, so she assumed that Blake had killed him in his sleep. But what about her babies? Had Blake killed them quickly as well? As much as the thought of her children dead made her feel like her heart had been shredded into a million tiny pieces, at least knowing that they had been killed in their sleep, unaware of what was happening, not afraid and not in pain, made it a little easier to cope with.

She squirmed again.

If she didn't get off this bed soon, she was going to lose her mind.

Just when she was sure that she would sell her soul to the devil—or to Blake Sedenker because, to her, they were one and the same anyway—the door opened.

Her confidence faltered. It was easy to think that she could offer up whatever Blake wanted to get herself out of this situation when she didn't actually have to do anything. But now Blake was back, and it was time to decide what her priority was. She could be stubborn, probably land herself a permanent place on this bed, or worse. Or she could at least try to play along, give him what he wanted, and pray that Agent Crane would find her eventually.

"Hi, honey, I'm home," he said happily like they were some old married couple in a family sitcom.

Swallowing her pride and her natural inclination to fight back, she said, "Hello, Blake."

He curled up his nose as he came closer to the bed. "You stink," he said bluntly.

"I'm sorry," she said immediately, feeling her cheeks heat in embarrassment. Was this going to make him angry? "I tried to hold on, but I couldn't." Violet waited anxiously to see his reaction.

Blake leaned over her, his expression inscrutable, but then he smiled and reached out to tenderly brush a lock of hair off her forehead and tuck it behind her ear. "Would you like a bath?"

She sighed in relief. "Yes, please."

"You'll be a good girl?"

Again, she had to swallow her pride. But she did it, forcing her lips to curl into something that vaguely resembled a smile. "Yes." It took a lot out of her just to utter that one word, but she did it and was rewarded by him untying the strips of the sheet from around her appendages. He then took her hand, helping her to her feet.

"I'd carry you, my love, but you're ..." he trailed off and gestured at her dirty and disheveled appearance.

"Th-that's okay," she answered immediately, thrilled to have escaped being cradled in his arms. She didn't want to do anything that was going to invoke any kind of intimacy between them. This was survival, pure and simple. She would do what she had to, but she didn't want to start letting herself feel anything for him other than anger and resentment for single-handedly destroying her life.

He kept hold of her hand as he led her through to the bathroom. The sight of it was heaven. She waited for him to release her so she could strip out of these clothes, dump them in the bath to wash them, then turn the shower as hot as she could stand and stay under there until she was as wrinkled as a prune and let the steam and hot water work their magic, soothing her so she could think clearly again.

But he didn't go anywhere.

He just turned the bath taps on then went about adding bath salts and bubble bath to the tub.

Maybe he was just going to run the bath and then leave her alone.

Again, she was wrong.

When the tub was full, he turned off the taps and then stood and faced her. "You can leave your clothes over there. When we're done, I'll run them through the washing machine and get you some clean clothes to wear."

He wanted her to undress in front of him?

That wasn't going to happen.

"Hurry up, Violet," he ordered. "After I bathe you, I'll cook dinner. I already have the roast in the oven, and I don't want it to burn."

After *he* bathed her?

She didn't want this man seeing her naked, and she certainly didn't want him touching her, but what choice did she have?

Afraid to anger him, Violet squeezed her eyes closed and shimmied out of her clothing before she could change her mind.

As soon as she was naked, he scooped her up and deposited her in the bath. The sweet smell of passionfruit—her favorite—wafted through the air. It was so creepy how he knew everything about her, right down to her favorite bath scent. He really thought that they were a couple. She would bet anything that the meal he was preparing was all of her favorites.

Blake picked up a loofah and poured her favorite body wash onto it, then he picked up one of her feet and began to wash her. Violet kept her eyes closed and tried to pretend that it was her husband's hands running up and down her body.

It didn't work.

He didn't feel like her husband; he didn't smell like her husband. The small groans he made as he lathered her up didn't sound like her husband.

Silent tears trickled down her cheeks, and she wished she was back in her ruined clothes on the filthy bed.

* * * * *

7:02 P.M.

Jett really wished that this was happening under different circumstances.

45

Getting to spend time with Savannah was exactly what he had wanted ever since they broke up, but not like this. He didn't want to be worried about her safety and wondering if his ex-partner was going to come after her. He just wanted to focus on winning her back. And he knew that was easier said than done.

"Hey, Fin. How's she doing?" he asked as he approached Savannah's hospital room.

"Better. Her temperature is back up to normal, and she's totally ready to get out of here."

No wonder. She'd been in the hospital for over a month after her first attack, and then another six weeks last Christmas. That was more time than any person should have to spend stuck in a hospital bed.

"Will she be going home today?" he asked.

"I think she'd sign herself out against medical advice anyway," Fin replied.

"Is that a yes?" With his ex-partner still out there and unpredictable, he had to make decisions about Savannah's safety.

"Yes. I was just about to go and discharge her. Then Chloe and I will take her home."

"That won't be necessary," he announced.

"Why?" Fin arched a suspicious brow.

"I'll be taking Savannah home." There was nothing the doctor, Savannah herself, or anyone else could say to change his mind.

"I don't think she's going to agree to that."

"She has a concussion, right?"

"Yes."

"So, she needs someone to keep an eye on her."

"Chloe and I can do that."

"And what if Blake decides to come back for her? Are you and Chloe going to take care of that too? Chloe is eight months pregnant, and you're a doctor."

"You really think he might come after her?"

"I can't know for sure, but it's possible."

"He let her go last night," Fin reminded him.

Blake had, and it was extremely out of character. Jett had been racking his brain to figure out why. The only thing he could come up with was that Blake had recognized Savannah. If he had remembered her, then that might have been enough for him to want to let her go. He knew Savannah. He knew what she'd been through and what she'd done. If there was anyone he would spare, then it would certainly be her.

But that didn't mean he wouldn't change his mind.

If there was one thing Jett wouldn't play around with, it was Savannah's safety. It didn't matter what the odds were that Blake would go after her—if there was even the smallest chance that he would, Jett was going to make sure she was protected every second of every day until Blake was caught or killed.

"I can't guarantee her safety. I'd rather be safe than sorry, so for the foreseeable future, she is going to have someone on her twenty-four-seven. I'm going to stay with her tonight, and then tomorrow, I'll organize someone to be with her while I'm at work."

"Maybe Tom could stay with her," Fin ventured.

"No, he has to stay with Hannah and the baby. Once Blake finds out that he's working this case, then it's possible that he'll go after Tom or his family."

"If Blake is going after everyone he perceives as a threat, then why hasn't he gone after you?"

"He has," Jett replied simply.

The first time, Blake snuck into Jett's house while he'd been at work and slipped cyanide into a bottle of water sitting in the refrigerator. If Jett hadn't had a top of the line security system—including cameras hidden in the ceilings of every room—then he would be dead.

The second time Blake had broken in, he had blocked Jett's chimney so when he lit a fire in the living room fireplace—which he did every evening in the winter—his house had filled with poisonous carbon monoxide. Thankfully, he had a carbon monoxide detector, but even with the warning, he'd inhaled enough of the gas to have to spend a day in the hospital.

He hoped there wasn't going to be a third time, but he wasn't so naïve to think that Blake wouldn't come after him again. They weren't partners anymore. Now they were adversaries, sitting on opposing sides of the fence. Neither was prepared to lose, but it was inevitable that one of them would. And now, with Savannah's life on the line, there was no way he was going to be the loser.

"You really think he's a threat to Savannah?" Fin asked.

"He's unpredictable, which makes him a danger to everyone he comes into contact with, but yes, I definitely think it's a genuine possibility that he may go after her."

"Okay, but she's not going to like the idea of you staying with her."

He huffed a mirthless chuckle. "Tell me something I don't know."

"Good luck."

"I'm going to need it."

Jett paused with his hand on the doorknob and took a moment to gather himself. He was ready for a fight. He knew that Savannah wasn't going to readily agree to let him stay with her, but he also knew she wasn't stupid, and she wouldn't unnecessarily put her life at risk.

He hadn't seen or spoken to her since he'd kissed her earlier this morning, and he wanted nothing more than to pick up where they'd left off, but Savannah wasn't there yet.

He opened the door and saw Savannah sitting in a wheelchair. Despite the fact that she'd been sitting in one the first time he'd met her, seeing her sitting in one again punched him in the gut. He hated that she had been hurt again. After everything she'd been through, she deserved some happiness, not more pain.

It'd been a year since the second assault; why wasn't she up and walking about? The first time, she'd worked day and night at physical therapy, determined to get back on her feet as soon as was humanly possible.

What was stopping her from doing that again this time?

If he had to guess, he would say it was fear.

Fear that she would fail, that she'd never be able to walk again. He knew how Savannah's mind worked, and he was sure that she preferred sticking with what she had rather than hoping for more and then not getting it.

"I hear you're getting out of here." Jett wasn't used to hanging back; he was accustomed to going after what he wanted and getting it, and right now, what he wanted was Savannah. It took every ounce of self-control he possessed not to just stalk over to her, pick her up, and take her home with him. Instead, he hung back. He knew being too aggressive was only going to further alienate her, and he was already going to make her angry when he informed her he would be staying at her place.

"As soon as Fin comes back with my discharge papers, he and Chloe are going to take me home," she said, watching him warily like she half expected him to go the picking-her-up-and-carrying-her-off route. She looked better than she had this morning. The deathly pale pallor was gone, and she now had a hint of color to her skin. Bruises were forming along one half of her face, and she was dressed in sweats and wrapped in two blankets.

"Actually, there's been a little change in plans," he ventured.

"What kind of change?" Savannah's blue eyes narrowed suspiciously, as did Chloe's brown ones.

"I'm going to be taking you home."

"Excuse me?" Savannah looked shocked and horrified by the very suggestion.

"My ex-partner is unpredictable. I'm concerned that by interfering with his plans last night, you may have become a liability he'll come back to extinguish," he explained.

"I can't believe it was Blake who kidnapped Violet," Savannah murmured. Blake might have recognized her, but she hadn't recognized him. She would have no reason to. Blake had changed a lot—both physically and psychologically since she had last seen him.

"I can't either," he said softly. Blake had been both his mentor and his friend, and to see what he had become was gut-wrenching.

"I'm sorry, Jett." She shot him a sympathetic look, but then it hardened. "But I don't get why that means you have to take me home."

"I'm not just taking you home—I'll be staying at your place until Blake is arrested."

Her eyes grew round as saucers, and her mouth hung open. "You're what?"

"I'm staying with you," he repeated, even though he knew she'd heard him.

"You're joking, right?"

"No. Your safety is not a joke."

"If Blake is dangerous and someone needs to babysit me, then why does it have to be you?"

Because he was in love with her, and there was no one else he trusted to keep her safe. And if playing temporary bodyguard also gave him an opportunity to wiggle back into her good graces, then he wasn't above using it. "Because this is just the way it is. Fin's coming to discharge you; I'll go bring the car around and meet you downstairs."

There was fear in Savannah's eyes, and he couldn't decide if it was because she was afraid that he would hurt her again, or because she was afraid that spending time around him would make her feelings for him bubble back up.

Jett hoped it was the latter.

* * * * *

8:13 P.M.

Savannah felt like her territory was being invaded by hostiles.

Okay, so the hostile was irritatingly hot and had once owned her heart, but still, she didn't appreciate Jett insinuating himself into her home or her life.

Her ex-boyfriend was the last person she had expected to find working Violet's case. She hadn't recognized Blake Sedenker last night, nor could she picture the man she remembered killing two people in cold blood and kidnapping someone. She didn't know what had changed him, and she didn't really care; she just wanted Jett to hurry up and find him so they could both go back to their lives.

Their *separate* lives.

She had absolutely no interest in entwining them together again. Now or ever. Jett was a part of her past, not a part of her future.

It didn't matter that Jett wanted to change that. He couldn't just walk back into her life after more than three years and kiss her.

Who did he think he was?

He didn't get to do that.

Not after how badly he'd hurt her.

She might have been the one who officially ended things between them, but if Jett had been there for her when she needed him, she never would have done it. She had been in love with him. Really and truly in love. She'd thought that they would get married, have kids, grow old together. She'd thought they would be together forever.

But he'd ruined it.

The one time she had needed him, *really* needed him, he hadn't been there for her.

Even after all this time, it still hurt.

She hadn't asked him for a lot—for anything, really. It wasn't in her nature to ask people to help her. She was one of those people who liked to do things for herself. But the one time she had asked him to be there for her, to support her, he hadn't been.

Jett may not have been there, but she had made it through that ordeal on her own, just like she had every other ordeal life had thrown at her. She had grown stronger, more independent, more determined, and now she didn't need him anymore.

"How come you haven't been going to physical therapy? It's been a year since you were hurt. I would have thought you would have been out of that thing in a month." Jett gestured at her wheelchair.

She groaned and ignored him, rustling through her bag to find her keys. She didn't want to discuss her assault with Jett. He gave up the right to play any part in her life when he abandoned her.

"I know you must be scared that you'll fail and won't walk again, but you can't give up. That's not who you are."

Darn him. Why did Jett have to know her so well?

"Did your doctors tell you that it was impossible for you to walk?"

Savannah opened the door and switched on the light, scooping up Sequin when the cat came running down the hall and rubbed against the front left wheel of her wheelchair. Purring and settling down in her lap, the cat waited to be wheeled down to the kitchen for dinner. They were routine people, she and Sequin.

"Have you spoken to your physical therapist from last time? I'm sure she'd be happy to work with you again," Jett said as he closed and locked her door behind them, then followed her down the hall.

"Aren't you supposed to be working?" she asked, lifting the bag of cat food out of the cupboard and pouring Sequin a bowl. "Don't you have to like, check that your crazy ex-partner isn't hiding out here somewhere waiting to kill me?"

"I had someone check the place out as we were driving here. If Blake had been here, I never would have brought you inside," Jett replied. "So maybe we could call her in the morning, make you an appointment."

He was relentless.

"I can go with you if you want," he continued, undaunted by the fact that she was clearly not interested in discussing this with him.

Savannah set the cat bowl on the floor, and Sequin jumped down to join it and began to eat in the most ladylike fashion. There was no rushing for her kitty cat.

"Do you still have her number? You should probably set up an appointment every second day for the first few weeks. Or maybe you remember all the exercises from last time. If you want, you can do some now, and I'll help you. I pretty much remember the drill, so even though I wouldn't be as good as having the physical therapist help you, it would be better than—"

"Stop!" she exploded.

Why was Jett doing this to her?

Couldn't he see that having him here was hurting her?

Why did he want to dredge up old memories when she was clearly not in a good place?

Did he get some sort of sick pleasure out of hurting her?

He knew how much she'd struggled to get through this last time because he'd been there. He and Blake were the FBI agents who had worked the case.

The man who attacked her had already abducted and killed six women across the country. That night, she had been having dinner with friends. She'd left before the others because she had to be at work early the next morning, so she'd been walking to her car alone.

That was when she heard it.

Muffled screams.

Then someone had called for help.

That word was like a siren reeling her in, and she had gone straight toward it.

She'd seen a man trying to drag a young woman through an

alley and into a car.

The man had been standing under a streetlight, and she had gotten a good look at him. That image was seared into her mind forever. It didn't matter how many years passed; she'd never forgotten him. He still haunted her dreams.

She had yelled at him to stop, and he'd turned and faced her.

That was all she remembered.

She had been found some time later beaten half to death.

Her hip hadn't been the only thing that had been broken. She'd had broken ribs, a broken arm, a fractured cheekbone, and a hairline fracture in her skull.

When she had woken up in the hospital more than forty-eight hours later, Jett had been the first thing she had seen. From the moment she had looked into those green eyes, she knew that they would wind up together.

Jett had been professional at first. He'd interviewed her and taken her statement. He'd been polite. He'd never touched her—not even a friendly handshake—even though her skin had burned for him.

Then the man who attacked her had been arrested.

The very next day, Jett had turned up on her doorstep and asked her out.

After that, they had been almost inseparable. He'd gone with her to physical therapy appointments, they'd spent holidays together, he'd slept in her bed and held her in his arms when she woke, screaming, from nightmares.

She'd loved him.

She'd let him get closer to her than any other living person.

She'd told him things about herself that no one else knew.

She hadn't just loved him; she had trusted him with every single piece of her, and then the day she had to appear in court to come face-to-face with the man who had nearly killed her and taken so much from her, he hadn't been there.

Jett had known how scared she was to see him again. She'd

had nightmares every night for a month. She'd had panic attacks every time she had to go and see the prosecutors; they did their best to prepare her for the vicious cross-examination they believed she'd be subjected to under the ruthless defense attorney who was representing her attacker.

He was supposed to pick her up from work the day before, but instead, another FBI agent had come to pick her up, delivering a message from Jett stating that he was sorry, but he wouldn't be able to make it to the court case.

She'd thought it must be some sort of joke.

Some sort of sick and twisted joke.

All night, she kept expecting him to come knocking on her door or use his key to her apartment to let himself in and come sliding into bed beside her.

But he never did.

She had lain awake waiting for him for hours before she finally cried herself to sleep.

She couldn't let go of the hope that he'd be there, though.

Right up until she was sitting in the courtroom being sworn in, she'd believed that he would be there for her. That he wouldn't make her go through this alone.

He had never come.

So, she'd sat there, unable to tear her eyes away from her attacker as she recounted the events of that night—grilled by the defense who was every bit as ruthless as she'd been warned.

Four days later, Jett had turned up at her door.

He'd been apologetic, *very* apologetic. All she had wanted to do was throw herself into those strong arms and sob against that rock-solid chest and let him take care of her and make everything better.

But she hadn't.

She couldn't.

All her life, ever since she had been a little girl, she had taken care of herself. Jett had been the first person whom she'd allowed to step into that role, and in doing so, she'd given him the power to crush her.

Knowing that was what had held her back from trying to fix things with Jett. She didn't want to be crushed. She didn't want love to destroy her. She couldn't do it. She didn't want to let him go, but fear had paralyzed her, and she hadn't been able to do anything else.

So, she'd told him to go.

Saying goodbye to Jett had been the hardest thing she'd ever had to do.

And now, he was back.

That desire to lean into him and let him hold her up was still there. Her skin still tingled with the need for him to touch her. His green eyes still brimmed with passion, and he still had the same smile and air of arrogance when he walked into a room.

He hadn't changed.

Neither had she.

That was the problem.

The fear of being hurt still left her barely able to draw a breath.

"Savannah?" Jett's voice tugged her from her thoughts. He was on his knees in front of her wheelchair, and he had a gentle grasp on her chin.

He was touching her.

So many emotions swirled inside her, so many words tried to come out that they clogged up her throat and got stuck.

His face was close to hers.

Too close.

When he was near her, she wanted so badly to find a way to forgive him. Maybe he had a good excuse for abandoning her. Maybe it didn't matter that he hadn't been there for her. Maybe she was blowing things way out of proportion.

"What are you thinking?" he asked softly, his thumb brushing lightly across her bottom lip.

Why couldn't he just go?

She couldn't think clearly when he was here.

His eyes were on her lips, and of their own volition, they parted. A fire started burning in her stomach, and it grew as he leaned toward her until she felt like she was about to spontaneously combust. She might still be angry with Jett, but her body obviously hadn't gotten the memo. It craved his touch, wanting nothing more than to have him inside her. It had taken control, ignoring her emotions and her mind. Her hands lifted, ready to curl around Jett's neck and drag him closer. She needed his lips on hers, she needed his hands on her body, she needed him like she needed her next breath.

Jett's lips met hers, and her brain snapped back into control.

Tears blurred her vision. How was it possible to crave someone and want nothing to do with them at the same time?

"Don't," she whispered.

Jett looked disappointed, but he immediately let go of her and stood. "Savannah—"

She didn't hear what he was going to say.

She just spun her wheelchair around and fled.

DECEMBER 22ND

2:24 A.M.

Why did he have to be so impatient?

He had pushed too hard too soon, and now he might have ruined any chance he had of getting back together with Savannah.

Jett couldn't sleep.

Instead, he was sitting in the dark in Savannah's living room, berating himself for moving too quickly. He just couldn't help himself. How could he be in the same room as her and not touch her, kiss her?

The simple answer was, he couldn't.

He wanted her. He saw nothing wrong with that, just like he saw nothing wrong with doing whatever it took to get her back.

She wanted him, too.

She could run from her feelings all she wanted, but it didn't change them. She was just afraid. But she couldn't live her whole life being afraid. In life, sometimes, you got hurt. He knew what she'd been through as a child and when she'd been attacked, and he knew it added to her fears, but she could trust him. He just wished she could see that.

Jett understood that because he'd let her down once before that, her trust in him had been shaken, but it wasn't fair to let one thing destroy everything they had shared. He would have explained to her where he'd been and why he couldn't be there for her if she would have just listened.

Maybe he should never have walked away.

Just because Savannah had said the relationship was over didn't necessarily mean it was so. She wasn't in charge, a relationship was fifty-fifty, he had a say as well. He should have made her listen. He should've refused to go. He should've done something—anything—other than just leave.

He'd only done it because he could see he had hurt Savannah badly.

But he never backed down, and he shouldn't have that time.

If Savannah thought he was going to leave her a second time, then she was sorely mistaken.

He was here, he was back, and he wasn't going anywhere.

Now, he just had to figure out how to convince her that them getting back together was a good thing and not the nightmare she seemed to think it was.

If nothing else, her body wanted him. More like, she was *desperate* for him. She had reacted to his touch. She'd been hungry for more, hungry for *him*. She had wanted him to kiss her; she'd wanted him to do more to her than just kissing. But fear had gotten the best of her. She had given him the ability to hurt her once before, and he had, so now she was scared of giving him that power over her again.

Savannah thought he didn't understand her, but he did.

He didn't know what it felt like to be so afraid of getting hurt that it paralyzed you, but he got that it was a big deal to Savannah.

Maybe he'd just go and check in on her. He had people watching the house, so he wasn't afraid of Blake getting to her tonight, but he was still glad to be here. He loved being around her even if he couldn't convince her to forgive him.

Quietly, he walked through the house and eased open her bedroom door. She'd closed it like by doing so she was shutting him out, but those days were over. She was sprawled out on the bed. In sleep, she looked even more beautiful as all the worry and weariness was gone.

As though she could feel his gaze on her, she whimpered and rolled over, lifting her bad leg as she went.

Jett was positive that if she would just give the physical therapy a try, then she would be back up and walking around again in no time. They both knew she would never have good use of the leg, but she could certainly get herself out of that wheelchair and back on her own two feet.

Even if he couldn't get her to forgive him and take him back—and while he believed he could, it killed him that he couldn't just order her to do it and be done with it—he was at least going to give her the courage to take those first steps.

He could do this forever. Just stand and watch her as she slept. When they'd been a couple, he'd often sat in bed and watched her. He wasn't someone who needed a lot of sleep. And since he'd met her just after she'd been attacked and she'd suffered from nightmares, he'd often lain awake, holding her tight against his chest, ready to calm her down if she woke in a panic. He wondered if she still had them.

Jett was debating moving closer, maybe even running a hand through that silky blonde hair. Sure, that was a little creepy, stalker-like, but he didn't really care—he loved her, and he wanted to touch her.

Just as he took a step, his phone buzzed in his pocket.

He pulled it out, and anger bubbled inside him.

He knew who it was.

Closing Savannah's bedroom door behind him, he returned to the living room then pressed answer.

"Watching her sleep?" a smug voice drawled in his ear.

Blake was outside somewhere. He'd send some of the agents watching the house to search for him, but they'd played this game before. By the time they found wherever he'd squirreled himself away, he'd be long gone.

"She's just as pretty as I remember," Blake goaded. "Blonde hair, blue eyes, those sexy pouty lips. Don't know why you ever let her get away."

His ex-partner knew exactly why he and Savannah had broken up.

"You back with her now?" Blake fished for information.

There was no good answer he could give to that question. If he said yes, it would make Savannah a bigger target than she already was. And if he said no and Blake suspected otherwise, then he wouldn't appreciate being lied to. He didn't want Blake thinking of Savannah at all.

"How's Violet?" Right now, Savannah was safe, but Violet Fisher wasn't. Blake might think that he was in love with her, but when she didn't do what he thought she should, he *would* hurt her. It was inevitable.

"Violet is fine, happy. We want to be together."

Now was not the time to correct his delusions, nor was he going to inform Blake that one of his intended victims had survived. Peta was recovering in the hospital, and as long as he didn't know she was still alive, then she would remain safe. Blake wanted to sever any and all ties Violet had to her old life, and if he managed to somehow find out the child was still alive, then he would definitely find a way to get to her and kill her. Even in the hospital, Peta wouldn't be safe.

"Stay away from us, Jett."

"You know I can't do that. It's not how you trained me. I can't walk away from this."

"I've already warned you, and you haven't listened. If you come near Violet, I'll go after the one thing you hold the dearest."

The bottom dropped out of his world.

Jett had known that Blake was a threat to Savannah, but hearing him confirm it still spiked fear inside him.

"You let her live last night," he said quietly.

"She's a victim; she wasn't a threat to me."

Blake was wrong there. Savannah wasn't a victim. She might have been victimized, but she was too strong and too determined not to be a victim. He just wished that she saw the strength she had inside of her that he saw. "Then nothing has changed. You don't need to threaten to hurt her, she's still not a threat to you."

"*Au contraire*. Now she's the perfect tool to use to finally get you to back off. Threatening you hasn't really worked so far—you're happy to risk your own life. But Savannah's, I don't think so. You're at her house right now. You're still in love with her, and you want her back. You mess with my woman, then I'll mess with yours."

Unfortunately, that was true.

He would gladly risk his own life to bring his ex-partner down, but putting Savannah in danger was a whole other story.

"Stay away from me and Violet, and I'll stay away from Savannah."

Jett wasn't sure he could do it.

He would do whatever it took to make sure Savannah stayed safe. Having officers drive by her house during the day and staying with her at night was no longer enough. She would need a bodyguard, and he would make sure he got her the best one.

But he wasn't walking away and leaving Violet in Blake's clutches.

He had promised to keep her and her family safe. He'd already failed them; there was no way he wasn't going to fail her as well.

Before he could tell Blake that he would never stop hunting him, that he would follow him to the end of the earth if that's what it took, that he would keep searching for him until he took his dying breath, the line went dead.

Blake thought he had outmaneuvered him, but he was wrong.

In their game of cat-and-mouse, Blake wasn't going to win—Jett was.

* * * * *

8:13 A.M.

It wasn't enough that Jett had invaded her home, but he had wormed his way into her dreams. All night Savannah had tossed and turned, dreaming about all the things that her subconscious wanted him to do to her.

So, her body and her subconscious had both already fallen for whatever spell Jett seemed to put her under. How much longer till her conscious mind betrayed her too?

Savannah dragged herself out of bed and into her wheelchair. As much as spending the day hiding under the covers appealed to her, she couldn't do that. Not while Jett was here. If she stayed in here, he was likely to come looking for her to find out what was wrong, and having Jett here in her bedroom might prove to be too big a temptation to resist.

She wheeled herself into her en suite bathroom to brush her teeth. She was a bit obsessive when it came to brushing her teeth. She brushed them as soon as she got up each morning, after every meal or snack—even after drinking anything but water—and right before bed.

As she brushed, she looked at her reflection. Long blonde hair tumbled over her shoulders, two old pale pink scars crisscrossed over each other on her forehead. Over time they had faded enough that if you didn't know they were there and weren't looking for them, you might not even notice them. Her eyes met her reflection's, and she stared deep inside them. She saw pain and fear. Is that what other people saw when they looked at her?

Is that what Jett saw?

Why was he suddenly so interested in reconnecting?

It had been nearly three years since they'd broken up, and he hadn't made any attempts to win her back, so why now?

Why did it hurt that he hadn't fought for her, for them?

She had been the one who decided to end things. He'd done exactly as she'd asked by leaving. She'd meant it when she told him it was over, so why did it matter that he'd listened? Had she really wanted him to ignore her and refuse to break up?

She was so confused.

It would be so much easier if she could just stay angry with

Jett.

Reluctantly, she had to admit that she wasn't anymore.

Hurt, yes, definitely.

But not angry.

Which made him even more dangerous.

Blake Sedenker may be able to kill her body, but Jett could do so much more. He could take her heart and break it into millions of tiny pieces.

She needed him out of her house.

The sooner, the better.

Like, right now.

Quickly running a brush through her hair, she went to her closet and pulled out a pair of tight-fitting jeans, a blue sweater that matched her eyes, and then a pair of her favorite boots to complete the ensemble.

Apparently, it was important to her subconscious that she look good in front of Jett.

Savannah debated adding makeup but stopped herself. She didn't want to give Jett the wrong idea. Okay, so, she wasn't mad at him anymore … And fine, her body craved him so much her mind couldn't stop conjuring up the images of all the things they could be doing if she'd only tell him yes … but she wasn't going to. She didn't want to get back together, and she didn't want to lead him on. He had hurt her, but she still believed that Jett was basically a good guy.

She rolled down the hall then came to an abrupt stop when she saw Jett, wearing one of her aprons—it was shaped like a gingerbread man—and standing at her stove cooking eggs and bacon.

The sight of him took her breath away.

He looked so sweet.

And ridiculously sexy.

She missed this. Having someone there when she got up in the morning, someone to talk to, someone to share things with, someone to care.

"Breakfast?" he asked, turning to shoot her a hundred-watt smile.

Snapping out of her trance, she joined him in the kitchen. "I hate breakfast," she said. If she ate before lunchtime, she always got a horrible queasy feeling in the pit of her stomach.

"I know." His grin grew wider. "I made you a smoothie. Mixed berry, your favorite," he said as he held up a glass.

She smiled in spite of herself. She didn't remember Jett being this sweet when they'd been together. He'd always been one of those guys who liked to take charge in everything he did. He treated her like a princess, but he wasn't really one for mushy sweet gestures like this.

Deliberately, she schooled her features back into a blank mask. Jett's smile faltered at her sudden change in demeanor, and she felt bad for hurting him. He had made his intentions clear. She owed him the same. "Thank you."

"Why haven't you done any baking?" Jett asked before she could ask him when he was leaving.

That was a conversation she wasn't interested in having.

With anyone, but especially with Jett.

"Savannah, what's going on?" His face and his tone suddenly went all serious. "This isn't you. You face things, even when you're scared. Not trying to walk again, that's bad enough, but now you're not even doing your Christmas baking. I don't understand. Talk to me."

He looked so concerned and so genuinely interested in knowing what was going on inside her head that she almost caved.

It would be so nice to have someone to talk to.

She had friends, and Chloe would certainly listen to anything she said and try to help in any way she could, but Chloe was finally happy and in love, married to the man she loved and awaiting the birth of their baby. After everything that had happened the first time around, she knew how worried both

Chloe and Fin were, and she didn't want to add to her friend's worries by burdening her with her problems.

"Are you baking your gingerbread masterpiece this Christmas Eve?"

"I wouldn't call them masterpieces," she protested immediately.

Ever since she was a very little girl, she had loved baking. One Christmas Eve when she was five, she'd asked her mom if they could bake homemade gingerbread men to leave out for Santa. That had been the beginning of her Christmas Eve baking tradition. Over the years, as she'd gotten older and more practiced, her creations had grown more elaborate.

Last Christmas, she had intended to make a fairground, including a gorgeous gingerbread carousel. She had planned it all out; she'd bought all the ingredients, and she'd made a few of the decorations that needed to be made early because they'd take too long if she did it all on Christmas Eve.

Then a couple of days before Christmas, she'd been attacked for the second time. She'd spent Christmas in the hospital, and by the time she finally got back into her own home, Christmas had been long gone, and there hadn't been any point in making it.

This year, she just wasn't in the mood to bake.

So she wasn't.

"Savannah?" He reached out to grasp her hand, but she quickly snatched it back.

"Your breakfast is going to go all disgusting if you leave it just sitting in the frying pan any longer," she said, making it clear that the topics of her walking, as well as her baking, were closed.

Jett dished up his breakfast, clearly disappointed that he couldn't get her to open up to him. He had no right to be disappointed. They'd broken up because she had been open with him about her feelings, and he had disregarded them and gone and done his own thing rather than be there for her.

This was too hard having him here.

She needed to get rid of him.

"So, I was thinking," she began cautiously, "that Blake probably isn't really all that interested in me. If he wanted me dead, he would have killed me when he had the chance. It's probably not really necessary for you to stay with me. If you're worried, you could always just ask the local police department if they can have a car drive past my house every couple of hours."

"Actually, Blake called me last night," Jett said gently.

"What did he say?" Savannah asked, but she already knew the answer. The look on Jett's face broadcasted it clearly.

"He threatened to come after you if I don't stay away from him and Violet."

"You'd never walk away and leave Violet with him."

"No, I won't."

He looked pained like she might blame him for putting her in danger, but she would never do that. She was the one who had gotten herself mixed up in this case. It was her fault that Blake had gotten his hands on Violet. And she loved that Jett was the kind of man who would do whatever it took to save someone who was counting on him.

"Blake is dangerous, and he's angry that I won't stop looking for him. He knows that I'm still in love with you, and he *will* use you to get to me. I thought staying here at night and having someone watch your house during the day would be enough, but it's not. From now until Blake is caught, you need a twenty-four-seven bodyguard," he announced in a tone that brokered no argument. "I wish it could be me, but I promised Violet that I wouldn't let Blake hurt her. I failed, and now I owe it to her to find her."

Jett looked conflicted about it, but to Savannah, it sounded perfect. She didn't want him around her at all, let alone permanently until this case was closed.

"If it's not you, then who's my babysitter?"

Before he could answer, her doorbell rang.

* * * * *

10:35 A.M.

She was biding her time.

Violet was playing along. She had let Blake bathe her yesterday, then she'd let him feed her, then handcuff her to him and sleep in the same bed. Well, she hadn't actually slept, she'd just lain awake trying to figure out a way to escape.

For now, she thought continuing to let Blake think that she was happy to be here with him and was going to do exactly what he told her was the safest idea. If he thought that he had her love and affection, then she might be able to gain his trust. And if she could gain his trust, then he might even let her go out on her own, thinking that she wasn't going to turn on him.

Only, he'd be wrong.

The first thing she'd do was find the nearest police station.

She wasn't sure she'd be able to last that long. She wanted out of here now. So far, Blake hadn't done more than touch her, but that couldn't last. Sooner or later, he was going to want sex, and that utterly terrified her.

Being stalked was one thing.

Being abducted was one thing.

Those she could handle.

But raping her, that took things to a whole different level.

One she couldn't cope with.

The only thing worse than being raped was knowing her family had been murdered. If she could, she would willingly have traded her body if it meant saving her husband and children.

Only, he'd never given her that choice, and now it was too late.

With her family already gone, she had nothing to lose. If Blake killed her, then there wasn't really anyone to miss her. With nothing to lose, she was going to take advantage of any and all opportunities that presented themselves.

At least he hadn't left her tied to the bed again. When he'd left her after bringing breakfast to her room and hand feeding her, he had connected the other end of the handcuffs that still hung from her wrist to a short chain. It didn't give her a lot of movement, and she couldn't even get to the bathroom, but, at least, she could move about a bit, and anything was better than being tied to the bed.

There was no clock in the room, and the curtains of the room's only window were drawn so she couldn't see out, but light peeked around the edges, so she knew that it was daytime. She had no idea where Blake was or what he was doing, but she hoped he came back soon. She desperately needed the bathroom.

Violet pressed her hands between her thighs and squeezed her legs together, trying to hold on. If Blake didn't get here soon, she was going to have to go in the corner of the room. She didn't want to do that; she was sick of feeling like an animal, forced to live in her own filth. Blake had changed the bedding after bathing her, but nothing could clean this room in her mind. The smell lingered in her nostrils, and she still felt it on her skin. No number of showers or baths were going to eliminate it.

The only thing that would was getting out of this room.

She wanted to fight back; she just didn't know how.

"Ugh," she groaned aloud.

She couldn't hold on any longer.

Violet was just moving into the corner and undoing the zipper on her jeans when she heard the key turn in the lock, and the door to her room swung open.

"I'm home, sweetheart. Did you miss me?"

She swallowed a string of insults and the desire to order him to let her go before offering him a sweet smile. "Yes. P-please, may I go to the bathroom?" She hated having to ask, but she wasn't so proud that she'd rather go in her pants.

"Of course," he said, nodding agreeably. He came and

unlocked the handcuff, then took her hand and led her to the bathroom.

When it was clear he intended to stay in there with her while she went, she shot him her most innocent look. "Please, may I have some privacy?"

For a moment, it looked like he was going to say no.

But then he smiled.

"I'll go and get a start on lunch. I hope I can trust you, Violet. I hope you understand why I brought you here and how much I love you."

"You can trust me," she lied, hoping she looked convincing.

She must have because he turned and left.

Violet could hardly believe her good luck.

Since she wanted to make sure he was really gone and off busy in the kitchen, and she really did badly have to go, she hurried to the toilet and did her business. Then once she'd washed her hands, she flew to the window. She had no idea where she was— once he'd shoved her into his car the night he had taken her, he'd given her something to make her pass out. She hadn't woken up until she was already here and stuffed in the closet.

When she threw back the blinds, she couldn't help but feel disappointed. She'd been hoping that they were in the city— somewhere where help would be just a few yards away—but they weren't. The only thing she could see was a huge expanse of grass and trees.

How was she going to get away?

It would take her several minutes to reach the relative safety of the tree line, and she had no idea where the kitchen was. Maybe it was on this side of the house and looked out on this same space.

She didn't have time to overthink; she didn't have time to worry; she didn't have time to come up with a better plan.

It was now or never.

Blake could come back at any moment, and although he was being all sweet and normal now, she knew he was an insane, unbalanced psychopath, and at any moment, he could turn on her. She didn't want to be here when he finally lost his composure.

Violet eased open the window and thanked her lucky stars that she was on the ground floor. She hated heights, and if she'd been on the second floor, she wasn't sure she would have been able to force herself to climb out the window and down the side of the house no matter how high the stakes were.

As soon as her feet hit the ground, she was off.

She ran as though her life depended on it.

Because it did.

She was maybe halfway to the trees when she heard a loud shout behind her.

Blake had seen her.

She might have lucked out to be on the first floor, but that luck hadn't continued to the kitchen being on the opposite side of the house to her bathroom.

As footsteps pounded on the ground, growing quickly closer, she quickened her pace. If she could just make it to the woods, she would be able to hide. If she could just dodge him long enough to find a road or another house, then she would be safe.

Her lungs were burning, her legs were quivering, but she didn't slow down.

She couldn't let Blake get her now. He would be furious. Violet was terrified to think about what he might do to her.

He was screaming something at her, but she couldn't make out the words. She didn't care what he was saying. All she cared about was getting to those trees.

She was almost there when his large body slammed into her, knocking her to the ground and landing on top of her, shoving the air from her lungs.

As she struggled to suck in enough oxygen to keep her heart beating, Blake flipped her over onto her back and straddled her stomach, pinning her to the ground. Pain hummed through her body, and she was sure she'd just gotten a new layer of bruises to add to the ones she'd gotten when Blake had thrown her against the wall yesterday.

"You think you can run away from me?" Blake roared. "You think you can leave me? You are mine. Mine!"

With that, he took one of her nipples between his fingers and pinched it so hard that she cried out at the sharp stab of pain.

It was over.

He was going to kill her.

She'd thought that she didn't care, that she had nothing to lose, and if he killed her, it would be no great loss. But now that she was staring certain death in the face, Violet realized that she wanted to live.

"You belong to me," Blake snarled. "I didn't want to sleep with you until you wanted it as much as I do. I understood that this has been a shock for you and that you need time to adjust to your new life. Don't you understand? I care about you. I love you. I don't want to hurt you, but you *are* mine, you belong to me, and I can take what I want from you. You best remember that next time you decide to try something stupid."

What?

He wasn't going to kill her?

"I can make your life better than you could ever imagine, give you everything you want, make all your dreams come true. Or I can be your worst nightmare."

Blake stood, dragging her up with him and threw her over his shoulder as he stalked back toward the house. Tears filled her eyes and trickled down her cheeks as the promise of safety from the trees got farther and farther away. Maybe she would have been better off if Blake had just killed her and been done with it.

* * * * *

10:35 A.M.

"It's only ten-thirty," Jett said to Tom.

Tom raised a questioning brow. "And?"

"That's about the hundredth time you've yawned already."

"My baby hates sleep," he explained with an eye roll, but couldn't hide the proud smile that spread across his face. It was clear his daughter already had him wrapped around her little finger.

Jett was thirty now and had thought by the time he reached this age, he would have been married with kids of his own. He'd thought he'd have those things with Savannah. He still did. He just had to convince *her* of that.

Kids had always been a part of his plan for his life. Jett had practically raised his six younger siblings after their father walked out on them.

One day he'd been a happy thirteen-year-old kid who had two loving parents, six annoying brothers and sisters whom he loved even when they drove him crazy. Hanging out with his friends and football had been the most important things in his life.

Then one day, they sat down to breakfast, and his father announced he was leaving.

Just like that.

No warning, no signs, nothing. His parents never argued much, and when they did, it never got out of hand. They seemed to get along; they held hands, kissed a lot, had date night once a month, and took the occasional romantic weekend away together.

They'd all been shocked when he made his big announcement.

No one more so than his mother.

When his parents divorced, his dad wanted nothing. He left everything to his ex-wife, including the kids. He didn't want joint custody of Jett and his siblings—he didn't even want visitation. He also didn't pay for child support because he'd simply disappeared.

With seven kids to raise and no one to help her do it, his mother had to work three jobs just to make ends meet. With his dad gone and his mom always at work, responsibility for the younger kids fell to him. His ten-year-old sister had helped out with chores and cooking, and the seven-year-old twins had helped to keep an eye on the four-year-old and one-year-old twins.

Life had been hard, and he'd had a lot to handle. While other kids his age were hanging out at the mall or going on dates, he was balancing his schoolwork with cooking, cleaning, laundry, changing diapers, heating bottles, and caring for his siblings.

As soon as he'd been old enough, he had taken on a part-time job so he could help financially contribute to the running of the family. His mom had wanted him to focus on school, but he couldn't let her continue to bear the burden of supporting the family alone.

Jett took his responsibilities very seriously.

Which was exactly why he hadn't been there for Savannah when she'd had to testify in court.

He'd wanted to be there more than anything. It had torn him up inside to know that she had to go through that alone, but he hadn't seen any other option. Sometimes there just wasn't any good choice to make, and you just had to go with your gut and do what had to be done, even if it ended up hurting someone.

"You want kids, Jett?" Tom asked.

"Yes," he replied immediately. He may not be a touchy-feely kind of guy, but he was always honest. He saw no reason to hide things or play games or pretend things weren't what they were.

"With Savannah."

It wasn't a question, but it was worth reiterating. "Yes. I know she's still pretty angry with me, but that hasn't changed my feelings for her. A relationship with her—a family with her—is still what I want."

"Don't give up hope. After Hannah and I got divorced, I was sure that it was really over. But then, when circumstances threw us back together, we got a second chance."

"Things between you and Hannah are a little different than

what happened with Savannah and me," he reminded Tom. "You and Hannah were victims. I deliberately chose to abandon Savannah right when she needed me the most."

"To save someone's life. I'm not pretending that if I were Savannah, I wouldn't have been hurt, but once you explain to her where you were and what you were doing, I'm sure that she'll understand."

"She doesn't want to hear it. It's too late. I left it too long. I was trying to do the right thing, honor her wishes, but I should have made her listen back then."

"It's not too late if she still loves you. I thought it was too late for Hannah and me. I thought that I'd been the only one who hadn't moved on, who was still living in the past, unable to forget about the only woman I ever loved. But she was stuck in the past too. When she named her jewelry store, she called it Sunkissed Jewels, a nickname that I came up with for her when we went on our first vacation together. She even used the date of that vacation for the security code for her safe ..."

Tom kept talking, but Jett had stopped listening.

Vacations.

He and Savannah had only taken one in the nearly eighteen months that they dated. He had taken her up to a cabin in the mountains in the middle of winter, and they'd spent the entire week curled up in front of the huge open fireplace making out and getting to know one another better. This was interspersed with a few walks through the quiet, snow-covered woods and romantic moonlit nights sipping hot chocolate on the porch.

That vacation had been as close to perfection as anything he had ever experienced.

It was that vacation where he had known for sure that he was in love with Savannah and that he wanted to spend the rest of his life with her. He'd even gone so far as to shop for engagement rings when they'd gotten home.

But then he'd gotten the call.

The one that had changed everything.

And when he'd gone rushing home to save the life of someone he loved, Savannah had gone to testify in court alone.

Jett still thought about that trip. He wondered if Savannah did too.

Sometimes those kinds of vacations were make-it-or-break-it events in a relationship. Being alone, secluded from the rest of the world where nothing exists but the two of you—it changed things, made you get to know the person in a whole different light.

If he could pick one thing from his past to go back to or to recreate, it would be that vacation with Savannah.

He wondered if Blake felt the same way.

He had already searched all the places that he thought his ex-partner might hide out, but he hadn't thought of a place where Blake and his ex-wife had experienced a magical vacation. Blake had Violet now, and he wanted her to love him as much as he believed that he loved her. Was it possible he was trying to recreate a holiday that he and Georgette had shared that had brought them closer together?

At this point, Jett was ready to try anything.

He yanked out his phone and dialed Georgette's number, one which he knew by heart after all these months.

"Who are you calling?" Tom looked confused.

"You just gave me an idea of somewhere to look for Blake," he replied as he waited for Georgette to pick up. "It's Jett," he announced the second she answered. "Is there any place special you can think of that you and Blake ever took a trip?"

"A trip?" she echoed.

"Something special. Just the two of you. Someplace where the two of you really connected and your relationship grew," he elaborated.

"There was a bed and breakfast," Georgette said slowly. "It was out in the woods, near some really beautiful hiking trails.

Before Laila was born, we went there a couple of times. It was the only place where Blake ever seemed to really relax and unwind, turn off work for a bit so it could just be the two of us," she said wistfully. Jett suspected that despite everything that had happened, some part of Georgette still loved Blake. "We conceived Laila there. He wanted to take her to visit, only we never got around to finding a time to do it because he was always working."

"What's the name of the bed and breakfast?" he asked. It didn't seem likely that his smart ex-partner would hide out with a kidnap victim at a bustling holiday destination, but with Blake, he wouldn't count anything out.

"It was called the Rest and Be Thankful Inn, but I think it closed down a couple of years ago. I remember, not long before all of this started, Blake wanted to go there for our anniversary, but when he called to make a booking, he found out the couple who ran it had passed away. Their kids couldn't decide what to do with it, so it was just sitting empty. He was really upset."

An empty bed and breakfast where Blake had been able to switch off work and enjoy quality time connecting with his wife was just the kind of place where he could be hiding out with Violet. "Text me the address," he told Georgette before disconnecting.

If Blake was really hiding out there, then he could have Violet home safe and sound with her daughter by the end of the day.

Then he could work on convincing Savannah to hear him out.

* * * * *

11:03 A.M.

"Would you please stop pacing?"

Savannah stopped her wheelchair and turned it to face her friend. "I can't pace, remember? I'm stuck in this thing."

"Rolling up and down the living room for the last two hours is definitely the equivalent of pacing," Chloe said calmly.

She glanced down at her legs. They were moving restlessly in her wheelchair like they wanted to get up and walk, annoyed at her for holding them back. For the first time since she had been attacked last Christmas, she wanted to get out of this chair and back up and walking.

If she hadn't been such a coward and wasn't still stuck in this thing, then Violet Fisher might not be the prisoner of a madman.

"It's not your fault," Chloe said.

Of course, it was.

She knew she'd messed up.

"You tried to stop it, and you were hurt. You could have died lying out there all night."

The dull throbbing headache she'd had since she woke up in the hospital yesterday morning and the bone-deep chill that she couldn't shake were constant reminders. But not reminders of how close she'd come to being killed; they reminded her of how badly she had failed.

"Stop blaming yourself."

"Then who should I blame?" she asked a little more vehemently than she probably should have, given Chloe was only trying to make her feel better.

"You should blame Blake. No one else is responsible for his actions. He's been trying to get his hands on Violet for months. Jett hasn't been able to stop him. How could you expect to?"

Chloe's comment was intended to help, but instead, it only made her feel worse.

How could she expect to help anyone while she was stuck in this thing?

"If I'd had my gun, I would have been able to stop him," she said, admitting what had been playing on her mind. "But I didn't. Because it would have taken me too long to go inside and get it, thanks to being stuck in this thing." She gave her wheelchair a glower. That she was still stuck in it only because she was too scared to try walking made her even angrier with herself.

"Why haven't you?"

"Why haven't I what?" she asked, keeping her gaze firmly fixed on her knees, avoiding her friend's probing eyes, as she knew exactly what Chloe was asking her.

"Why haven't you tried to walk?" Chloe asked, patiently.

Fear.

Fear of failing.

Fear of letting people down.

Fear of letting herself down.

Instead of telling Chloe any of that, she took the coward route and said nothing.

They sat in silence for several minutes, tension crackling beneath the surface. Savannah didn't want to argue with her friend, but she wasn't ready to discuss her fears with anyone yet.

Her gaze landed on the Christmas tree. She hadn't wanted to put it up this year, but Chloe was all excited and full of Christmas spirit and had insisted on them decorating together. Savannah got it; last Christmas, Chloe had gotten her life back, and now she and Fin were happy and expecting a baby. Chloe believed that Christmas magic was to thank, so this year she was going all out. If Chloe and Fin hadn't turned up at her door on December first with a tree, she probably wouldn't have bothered with the holiday season at all.

While she'd gone along with the tree, she hadn't done any Christmas baking. Usually, by now, just a couple of days away from Christmas, she would have baked dozens of different things and been busy preparing for her big Christmas Eve gingerbread creation. She never ate much of it herself—there was just too much for one person to eat—so she usually gave it away to family, friends, colleagues, and neighbors.

So far this Christmas season, several people had asked her why she hadn't baked, and while she knew they were all disappointed, she just had no motivation whatsoever to make anything.

As she looked at the tree, all full of twinkling lights and sparkly decorations, it seemed so out of place. Her life was anything but twinkly and sparkly right now. One decoration, in particular, caught her attention. It was a small piece of wood in the shape of a star. On it was a carved scene of a cabin in the snowy woods with a couple standing hand in hand. Jett had carved it for her from a piece of wood they'd found when they'd spent a week at a secluded cabin in the woods just like the one in the scene.

A smile crept across her lips as she remembered that trip. Curled up in Jett's arms in front of the roaring fireplace; talking for hours on end, learning every little detail about each other; strolling through the snow-covered woods and Jett carrying her on his back when the snow got too deep for her to walk through; sitting on the porch sipping hot chocolate as snowflakes fluttered through the air. That trip had been magical, and by the end of it, she had known for sure that Jett was the only man for her.

She just wished that things had gone differently, that they hadn't gotten all messed up. She wished Jett had stayed out of her life instead of coming back into it and playing with her feelings all over again.

How could she want someone so badly, her body craving him, but at the same time, dread seeing him?

Maybe she shouldn't have tortured herself by keeping the decoration Jett had made for her. She had contemplated leaving it behind when they broke up, but she just hadn't been able to. Part of her had needed to hold onto it, needed to maintain some connection to him.

"Fin's snowman briefs arrived," Chloe announced.

Despite her morose mood, Savannah couldn't help but laugh. "What?"

"You know how I love to wear crazy Christmas clothes?"

"Like that Christmas tree sweater you're wearing right now," she pointed out, smirking.

"Right." Chloe grinned. "Well, last Christmas Eve when Fin and I had sex for the first time since we broke up, I was wearing these panties with a snowman face. Well, let's just say Fin had some fun removing them. So, I ordered him a pair so that I can have just as much fun. I was worried they wouldn't arrive in time, but they made it."

"Chloe!" She couldn't help but laugh at her friend's blatant attempt at lifting the mood with her way-too-much-information story.

"Give Jett a chance, Sav," Chloe said, growing serious. "You don't have to take him back if you don't want to, but at least give him a chance to explain. As hard as it is to hear, maybe he had a good reason why he couldn't be there for you. If you still love him, then I think you owe him the chance to explain."

Was Chloe right?

She *did* love Jett. She had before, and while she might have buried those feelings after they split up, they were still there.

Maybe she should give him a chance to tell her why he hadn't been there. It didn't mean she had to get back together with him, but she could at least hear him out. There was no harm in that, right?

Chloe's phone buzzed, and she picked it up, her face going grim as she read whatever message she'd received.

"What's up?" Savannah asked.

"It's nothing."

The tone of Chloe's voice clearly indicated it wasn't nothing. "Chloe? What's going on? Is it something to do with Blake?"

"No, nothing to do with Blake."

"Marcus King." There was nothing else it could be. "You're still keeping tabs on him."

"Trying to," Chloe agreed. "He hasn't made contact with his PO since he was released, but he doesn't seem to have taken more victims."

"Well, that's good," she encouraged. Marcus King was a child rapist and murderer who had been jailed for sixteen years before being released a year ago.

"I guess so." Chloe looked conflicted. She wanted him back in prison, but the only way to get him there was for him to take another victim. That meant another child had to be raped and murdered, another family torn to pieces, for Marcus King to be put back where he belonged.

"At least he hasn't come after you." Chloe's testimony had been what put Marcus King behind bars, and at the trial, he had sworn vengeance on her, but twelve months had passed since the man had been released, and he hadn't made any contact.

"I just wish he was still in prison." Chloe rested a hand on her pregnant belly. "I don't want my baby born into a world where Marcus King is a free man. I know it's stupid. I know there are hundreds of rapists and pedophiles and killers out there, but …"

"But none of them had any contact with you," Savannah finished. She couldn't imagine what it would be like to bring a baby into the world when you spent your days dealing with crime and criminals and victims. At one time, she'd thought she and Jett would have kids, but now she wasn't sure of anything. She'd thought she and Jett would have a family, but then she'd resigned herself to a life alone, and now that the possibility of a reconciliation with Jett was tantalizingly close, she just wasn't sure if it was what she wanted or if it was what was best for her.

* * * * *

12:47 P.M.

Finally, everything was in place.

It had been a long two hours.

Ever since Georgette had told him of the now-closed bed and breakfast, all Jett had wanted to do was drive as quickly as he could to the old house and arrest his partner. But he had to play this carefully. Blake was smart and one wrong move and the man would slip through his fingers again, taking Violet with him.

There were still no guarantees.

He couldn't go all out and bring in the entire FBI—much as he might want to—because that would be sure to tip Blake off, but he had what he hoped was enough agents to end this. He just had to hope that for once, Blake wasn't entirely unpredictable. So far, his unpredictability had, in fact, been the only thing predictable. No matter what he tried, his ex-partner always seemed to be one step ahead.

Not this time.

This time, he was walking away the winner.

Violet's life depended on it.

Savannah's, too, and there was nothing he wouldn't do to ensure her safety.

Jett wished that he could spend some time watching the place, confirm whether Blake was here, see if he could figure out which rooms Blake was using and where they would likely find him as well as which escape routes he might use. The longer they stayed and waited, the riskier it got. Blake could have a surveillance system set up. He could already know they were here and possibly be preparing to run.

Without as much knowledge as he would have liked in order to be properly prepared, Jett, Tom, and the half dozen agents with them parked their cars in the woods on one side of the house. He was hoping that if they kept the cars out of sight, then maybe they could keep the element of surprise on their side.

Unfortunately, the house was set in the middle of a grassy clearing. There was no way they could approach without being seen. If Blake was in there and anywhere even vaguely close to a window, he would see them. The best they could hope for was to surround the house and trap Blake inside.

Jett's concern about that was that he believed his ex-partner would rather die than go to prison.

That, in and of itself, didn't necessarily bother him. He'd liked Blake. The man had been his mentor and his friend, and he hated what he had become and wished there was something he could do to undo it, to turn Blake back into the man he'd been before. But he had accepted that that wasn't to be. And if Blake wouldn't stop, then he was a danger to society, which meant there were only two options—prison or death. And while Jett would prefer for Blake to go to prison, if he chose death, then at least he would no longer be a threat to Violet or anyone else.

The only problem was if Blake felt like he was backed into a corner and there was no escape, then he wouldn't just kill himself, he'd kill Violet too. He was definitely an "if I can't have her, then no one can" kind of guy.

Once they had Blake surrounded and trapped in the house, then maybe there was a chance that he could talk his ex-partner down. He wasn't sure how, but he had to believe that somewhere deep inside, part of the man he'd known before still existed.

He just hoped that Blake didn't decide to shoot first and ask questions later. He wouldn't put it past the man to shoot them off one by one as soon as he saw them approaching. Blake had the advantage—he was safely tucked away inside the house and completely covered; they would be unprotected and out in the open as soon as they stepped out of the relative safety of the trees.

It was now or never.

Things weren't going to get any better or safer.

At Jett's nod, they all spread out with their guns drawn so the house would be surrounded, cutting off any attempts at escaping Blake might make.

Jett's heart was thumping, adrenalin buzzing through his system. Although he knew the stakes, he couldn't deny that he lived for this. The thrill of closing in on a dangerous killer, the high of the catch—it was what had drawn him to the FBI in the first place, and even after years of doing this, that rush hadn't dimmed.

They were almost to the house when he sensed something behind him.

Whatever it was that made him turn around was a godsend.

Blake emerged from the tree line.

Violet was right behind him. Her arms were out in front of her, tied up at the wrists, and a rope looped from her bound wrists to Blake's hand. He was leading her around like his pet, and in some ways, Jett believed his ex-partner thought of her that way. Violet was a thing that he wanted to own, to dominate, to control, and once he got bored of playing with her, he was going to kill her.

He froze.

Blake caught sight of them, and he stopped.

For a moment, their eyes met.

So much passed between them in those few seconds.

Their gazes battled for control, neither of them willing to give an inch.

Time seemed to stop for a moment, then all of a sudden, it sprang back to life. Blake snatched Violet up and threw her over his shoulder, then he darted back into the woods in the direction from where he'd come.

"Over there," Jett yelled to the others as he took off after Blake.

Not bothering to see if the others were following him, he sprinted toward the woods. He couldn't let Blake get away. He pushed himself to catch up, knowing that Blake could have a car hidden somewhere or someplace to hide out.

They must have been out hiking. He should have predicted that. Georgette had said that one of the things that she and Blake had done when they stayed here was go out on hikes, so it made sense that he would take Violet out to the same places he had spent time with his ex-wife.

He broke through the tree line and headed in the direction he believed Blake had run, the others just behind him. "Spread out," he ordered. Blake had a good hundred yards' head start, but he was carrying Violet, which would slow him down and give them a chance to catch up.

For several minutes, he ran blind. He had no idea if he was going the right way or if Blake had managed to win again and make it to freedom. Jett was about to give up when he spotted movement.

"Blake, give yourself up," he shouted.

"Never," a voice yelled back.

"You're outnumbered." He tried to reason with Blake, even though he knew it was impossible. You couldn't reason with an irrational human being.

"You'll never get me, Jett. You should've listened and stayed well enough away," Blake said, his voice a mixture of cockiness and threatening.

Just as he broke through the tree line once again, this time to find himself on the shore of a large river, an engine revved loudly. Blake had dragged Violet onto a boat and was taking off across the river. There was no way he'd be able to catch him now. That left him with only one option.

"I don't want to shoot you, Blake," Jett said, almost pleading with his ex-partner. He had killed before when he'd had no other choice, but he didn't want to kill Blake.

Blake yanked Violet up across his body, using her as a human shield.

There was no way he could get a clean shot, and Blake and Violet were getting farther away with each passing second. In another couple of minutes, they'd be across the river and disappearing into a car Blake no doubt had lined up and waiting should his hideout be discovered.

Even from here, Jett could see bruises marring Violet's pale skin, and earlier in the clearing, she'd been walking awkwardly like she was in pain. Blake had already hurt her; he didn't know how much longer she could survive as his prisoner. Blake might think he loved Violet, but the only person he loved was himself. In the end, he would just hurt Violet over and over again, trying to force her to reciprocate his feelings before he killed her.

"Please, Blake," he tried one last time. "Think of Laila. Think of your daughter. She loves you, and she deserves a father who can be there for her. Don't make her bury you. Don't make the final memories she has of you be this. Come back with me, get help, let Laila keep her daddy."

The boat didn't slow down, and it was already three-quarters of the way across the river now.

He couldn't get a clear shot at Blake.

So, Jett aimed at the next best thing.

* * * * *

1:10 P.M.

Jett actually did it.

A loud bang sliced through the air, and then the boat shuddered violently.

He had fired at them.

The boat was flimsy at best, and the single bullet was enough to pierce a hole through the side and water promptly sank the small craft.

Both he and Violet were plunged into the icy water.

For a moment, it stole his breath and his ability to move as his muscles seized up at the sudden dramatic drop in temperature.

The pull of the river yanked him under, and the second his lungs were deprived of oxygen, he snapped out of his dazed stupor and kicked his legs, propelling himself back up to the surface.

Jett hadn't been alone. He had counted seven other agents. He was outnumbered, but there was enough distance between him and Violet and the others for him to still get away.

Violet.

Quickly, he scanned the water for her, but he didn't see her.

If she'd suffered the same momentary shock as they'd hit the freezing water that he had and been pulled under, then with her hands tied together, she might not have been able to swim herself back to the surface.

Frantically, he began to search the water for her. Every precious second counted right now, but he couldn't let her drown. Without her, he had nothing.

Blake dived down. He and Violet had been right beside each other when the boat sank. She couldn't have gone far—the currents in the river weren't that strong.

He was about to give up hope when something brushed across his hands.

Hair.

He curled his fingers around it and pulled.

A moment later, both his and Violet's heads popped up above the water's surface.

There was no time to check that she was all right; he had to believe that she was. If only she hadn't been stubborn, then he never would have had to restrain her. This was all Violet's fault, and when he got them out of here, she was going to be punished for it.

He didn't enjoy punishing her, but this morning he had taught her who was in charge here. He had claimed every part of her, taking her so hard she'd be sore for days, leaving bruises that would take weeks to fade, and scars that would remind her every day for the rest of her life that actions had consequences. When you went against the one who loved you, it caused you both pain.

As unpleasant as this morning had been, he knew that sometimes a swift and well-executed punishment was necessary. Now Violet would think twice about disobeying him. He was not going to wind up with another Georgette on his hands. That impudent woman had taken his child from him—his own flesh and blood—and thought nothing of it. There was no way he was going through that again. Violet would learn to obey him; anything less than that was not an option.

Voices were shouting behind him, but Blake paid them no heed. He knew it was just Jett trying to get him to stop and yelling out orders at his colleagues.

He didn't care what Jett was yelling about.

His ex-partner thought he was going to wind up victorious, but he kept forgetting who had trained him. Blake had taught Jett everything he knew, and therefore, he knew exactly what moves Jett was going to make before he made them. You didn't spend half your life working for the FBI and not know how to beat them at their own game.

Hooking an arm around Violet's chest, he swam toward the shore. She struggled in his grip, which both confirmed she was alive and irritated him. Why was she always fighting him? He didn't understand it. He loved Violet; he wanted to give her everything, and he wanted to spend the rest of their lives making her happy. What was so wrong about that?

Maybe he shouldn't have killed her family, but as long as they were alive, she was never going to truly be his. She was always going to want to go back to her kids. He knew because he still missed his daughter with every fiber of his being. Georgette could take Laila away and keep her from him, but she could never stop him from being her father. And as long as Violet's children were alive, she would always be their mother. With the children out of the way, she was free to be his and only his.

No one was going to take her away from him.

The water grew shallower, and seconds later, he was climbing out of the cold water and up onto the bank. Afraid that Jett might try shooting at him again, he quickly snatched Violet up into his arms and darted back into the safety of the trees.

His heart rate slowed once they were out of the open.

They were safe.

For now, at least.

He just had to make sure they stayed that way.

He had at least ten cars hidden in the vicinity, and one was nearby, only a hundred yards or so through the woods. If he could get to it, they'd be out of here before Jett and the others ever made it over to this side of the river.

Blake had a backup plan and a backup plan for his backup plan and a backup plan for his backup plan of his backup plan. Since he'd been stripped of his job, he had nothing to do but sit around all day and plan out how to get what he wanted, and now that he had it, it was time to disappear.

His legs were heavy, and the water-laden clothes plus Violet's weight slowed him down, but adrenalin was coursing through his system. It lent him extra strength and energy when he would otherwise have depleted his reserves, and he made it to the car in just a couple of minutes.

He set Violet down and ran to a tree, quickly climbing halfway up to where he had hidden the key.

As soon as she was free of him, Violet scrambled to her feet and started to run.

Cursing under his breath, Blake took off after her.

She was just stacking up punishment upon punishment.

When he caught up to her, he made sure to slam his entire body weight into her, sending her sprawling to the ground, gasping as the wind was knocked from her lungs.

"Stop running," he hissed as he picked her up before she could catch her breath and try to escape once again. He carried her back to the car and popped the trunk. "You can't be trusted, then maybe I should just keep you in here until you learn your lesson," he threatened.

Only, he knew he wouldn't follow through on that threat. He couldn't stand to be far away from her for long. He loved the feel and taste of her body, and he needed her close, not locked away in the trunk of his car.

"You're lucky I love you so much," he said, his tone softening. He couldn't really stay angry with her for long. When he punished her, it was only out of love. A love he wanted her to reciprocate. A love he *would* get her to reciprocate.

He cupped her cheek with one hand, his other stroked her wet brown locks. She stared up at him with her huge violet eyes. She was trembling, her usually pale skin even paler than usual. He needed to get her warmed up. Leaning over her, he touched his lips to hers, kissing her gently, lovingly, the opposite of the way he'd treated her when they'd been together earlier today.

Blake slammed the trunk closed and climbed into the driver's seat, then he sped off to one of his safe houses.

This had gone on long enough.

He wasn't playing this game any longer.

Jett wanted to take Violet from him, so he would take Savannah from Jett. See how he liked someone messing around in his relationships.

He had thought that Jett and Savannah had split up. She'd been angry and hurt that Jett had to go home and take care of something instead of going with her to court when she testified. Jett had been heartbroken but too stubborn and stupidly noble to make Savannah listen to him explain why he hadn't been there.

Personally, Blake had liked Savannah, thought she was tough and smart, and not afraid to do the right thing even if it put her in danger. He didn't want to hurt her, much less kill her, but Jett wouldn't listen to reason. He'd asked his ex-partner politely to stay away from him and informed him of the consequences. Jett had chosen not to listen. What happened next was on Jett's head. He would have no one to blame but himself for the death of the woman he loved.

* * * * *

6:22 P.M.

The doorbell rang, and Savannah lifted her head.

"Aren't you going to get that?" she asked when her bodyguard made no move to get up off the couch.

Sawyer just grinned at her. "You can answer the door."

"I thought that was what you were here for. I'm the one who's been threatened; I'm the one who's apparently in danger. What if it's him? You want me to answer it and just hand myself over to him on a silver platter? And why are you smiling at me like that?" she asked her twin brother. She shouldn't have been surprised that Jett had called her brother and asked him to babysit her until Blake Sedenker was caught. Sawyer was a bodyguard, good at his job, and Jett knew she would be more comfortable with her family than she would with a complete stranger. She was touched that he'd done that rather than just letting whatever agent the FBI assigned to her watch over her.

"Go get the door, Sav." Sawyer was still smiling at her, and she got the feeling he knew exactly who was at the door.

Confused, and a little apprehensive, she moved from the couch into her wheelchair. Sawyer didn't move to help her, not because he didn't want to—because she could clearly see by the way his hands were curled into fists and resting on his knees that he wanted nothing more than to scoop her up and deposit her in her chair, so she didn't have to do it herself—but because he knew she liked to be independent.

She wheeled out of the living room and tentatively raised a hand to the doorknob, hesitating before she turned it. Who was on the other side? Why did Sawyer want her to open the door? Why all the mystery?

Slowly she opened the door, and her mouth fell open in surprise.

Jett stood there, wearing a pair of jeans that showed off his muscled thighs, and a gray sweater that hugged his body and highlighted his perfectly sculpted chest. His green eyes twinkled merrily, and his scruffy beard made him look ridiculously sexy.

There was a possibility she just drooled a little bit.

"Good evening, Savannah," he said formally, but his smile was amused.

He leaned in to kiss her, and her lips parted, her breath caught in her throat, her face lifted up to meet his. Then his lips touched ...

Her cheek.

Her cheek?

Was she disappointed?

She was.

She'd *wanted* him to kiss her.

It was probably just because she hadn't had sex since they broke up. And he *was* very attractive. Plus, add in lingering leftover emotions, and she was sure that was all it was.

Just because she had decided to give him an opportunity to explain to her what had happened two and a half years ago that prevented him from supporting her in court, that didn't mean she had to take him back.

"I brought you these," Jett said, drawing her attention away from his lips and the longing her own felt to have them on her. "And these." He held out a bouquet of roses and a box of chocolates—her favorites.

What was he doing here?

And with gifts?

Sawyer had obviously been expecting him, so the two of them had arranged something, but what?

"Why are you here?" Savannah asked. She realized she sounded a little blunt, but she didn't like her brother and her ex discussing her behind her back.

Jett didn't look fazed by her semi-rude tone. "I'm here to take you out on a date."

A date?

With Jett?

A date with Jett?

Savannah groaned inwardly. Why was she asking herself so many questions? She should be asking Jett those questions.

"A date?" she asked.

"Dinner. If you'll come with me," he added, a tiny glimmer of doubt in those gorgeous green eyes.

It was time to decide.

She could keep being a coward and hiding behind her pain and fear and this wheelchair. Or she could give Jett a chance. This didn't have to mean anything. It could just be dinner.

"Thank you." She smiled, taking the flowers and the chocolates, and setting them on her lap. "I'll just go and change."

"Don't bother, what you're wearing will be fine," Jett told her, his easy smile back in place now that she had agreed to the date.

She looked down at what she was wearing. She had on PJ pants and an old sweatshirt; she was hardly dressed to go out to dinner. "Really? This is okay for wherever you made reservations?"

Jett grinned. "Trust me, it's perfect. Let's go."

In somewhat of a daze, she allowed Jett to pluck the gifts he'd brought from her hands and pass them off to Sawyer, then took control of her wheelchair and rolled her down the drive. Usually, she would never let anyone push her wheelchair, but Jett wasn't like her brother; he wasn't worried about offending her by taking over.

At the car, he didn't wait to ask first, just slipped his arms under her knees and behind her back, picked her up, and deposited her in the passenger seat.

The ride to wherever they were going was quiet. Neither of them felt completely comfortable with the other—it had been so long since they'd been a couple that being together again felt awkward. Good, but awkward.

Good.

It really *did* feel good to be around Jett again. She'd missed him. She might not have let herself think about him because it was so painful, but she really had missed Jett. A lot.

Savannah wanted to say something to ease the tension, but she wasn't sure what.

"Your house?" she asked when Jett finally parked the car. "We're having dinner at your place?" It made sense since he'd told her not to bother about how she was dressed. But given that Blake had threatened to hurt her to get Jett to back off, being at his house didn't seem like the smartest place to be. Surely Blake wouldn't go after them in a crowded restaurant. "Are we going to be safe here?"

"I wouldn't let Blake hurt you." Jett looked offended by the very notion.

"I know you wouldn't," she assured him, and honestly believed it to be true.

"See that car over there?" he asked, gesturing to a white sedan farther down the street. "There are agents inside. And that house across the street." He paused to point out the house. "There are agents in there, too. You're safe here, Savannah." He turned back to her. "You're safe with me."

She knew he meant more than just physically safe. He meant she was safe to open up to him. That she could tell him what was scaring her and why she hadn't tried to walk again. Savannah wasn't quite ready to go there yet. Spending some time with Jett, even going on a date with him, was one thing, but she wasn't ready to put her heart on the line and bear her soul this quickly.

Instead, she just smiled at him. "I'm excited to see what you have planned for dinner."

He smiled too. He didn't seem upset that she wasn't ready to talk. He looked like he knew he had to work to regain her trust and was prepared to do so. He'd said from the first time he saw her again that he wanted her back, and Jett always meant what he said.

"I'll grab your wheelchair, and you can go and find out."

Again, he didn't bother asking; he just grabbed her chair, then opened her door and picked her up, setting her down in it.

As soon as he pushed her inside his front door, she knew what dinner would be.

Jett had a fire raging in the fireplace, and he'd piled up blankets and pillows on the floor in front of it. A large garland strung with fairy lights framed the fireplace, and Jett's Christmas tree was beside it, decorated to the hilt.

Minus the Christmas decorations, this was exactly how they had spent their days in the cabin on the vacation she'd been thinking about earlier.

"Dinner is s'mores," she said softly. It was both her and Jett's favorite, and they'd had them every day at the cabin.

"There are also chocolate chip cookies, shortbread, white Christmas, snowballs, fudge, sugar cookies, truffles, candy, cinnamon rolls, and peanut butter balls."

"Everything that I usually bake in December."

"Except for the gingerbread." The look in Jett's eyes said he had other plans for that. "I was thinking about the trip we took—
"

"Me too," she interrupted. "I was looking at the decoration you made for me."

"You still have it?"

"Of course." She wasn't going to tell him that she had considered throwing it away on more than one occasion. "Jett, this is—this is perfect," she finished breathily.

"You want to go sit down?"

All she could do was nod. Right now, she wanted to do a whole lot more than just sit and talk to Jett. This time she hoped he'd pick her up and carry her in his strong arms.

She wasn't disappointed.

Now that she was thinking clearly, she curled an arm around Jett's neck and snuggled closer. Since she had met Jett after she'd been attacked and because he was such an alpha sometimes, he had carried her around quite a bit in those early days of their relationship. Maybe it wasn't very "modern woman" of her, but she loved being cradled in the arms of the man she loved. It made her go all gooey inside to think of how strong he was and how safe she was with him.

"I missed you, Savannah," Jett said, his breath tickling the sensitive spot behind her ear. A spot he *knew* was a sensitive one for her. A spot that always left her wanting more. "I should never have walked away."

If Jett had stayed and tried to pressure her to stay together back then, it probably wouldn't have made a difference.

But now that he was back, maybe for good, maybe things could go back to the way they'd been before.

It all depended on what reason he gave her for not being there.

"What do you want to eat first?" he asked as he sat her down on the mountain of blankets and tucked one around her.

"S'mores," she replied immediately.

"S'mores coming right up."

Savannah watched Jett as he held the two sticks in the dancing red flames. There were so many things she wanted to ask him, so many things she wanted to tell him. Two and a half years was a long time, and they had so much catching up to do.

Before they could do any of that, though, she needed to know.

It couldn't be that bad.

He *must* have had a good reason.

He wouldn't have made her do that alone unless he had no other choice.

With the Christmas tree and the twinkly lights, everything looked so beautiful. Magical, even. Why couldn't Christmas magic just fix things between the two of them? Last year Chloe and Fin had gotten a Christmas miracle. Why couldn't she and Jett get one this year? This was the time of year where love and hope reigned. She wished that they could just make everything better, but she knew it didn't work that way. The only thing that could fix what she and Jett had broken was a lot of hard work.

"Where were you, Jett?" she asked as soon as he sat down beside her and handed her a s'more.

He reached out an arm and draped it across her shoulders. She didn't shrug out of his grip, but she didn't snuggle closer either. She couldn't yet. Not until she got her answers.

"Someone I grew up with got into some trouble—trouble she couldn't get out of on her own. She started taking drugs, got addicted, and she didn't have enough money to buy, so she got into dealing. Dealing led her to gangs, and before she knew it, she was in deep. A raid was going down, and I got wind of it through an old friend who recognized her name. I knew the gang she was with, and they weren't going to go quietly; they would rather go down in a bevy of bullets than get arrested. I had to get her out. I couldn't let her die, Savannah." With his free hand, he grasped hers and squeezed it tightly. "That didn't mean it didn't kill me that I wasn't there for you."

Her heart melted a little.

It still hurt that Jett hadn't been there when she needed him, but she now understood why he hadn't.

"You should have told me." She squeezed his hand back. "I would have told you to go."

He kissed her temple. "You're right. I should have. I'm sorry I didn't."

"Did you get her out?"

"Yes. We may have broken a couple of laws along the way, but we got her out before the raid went down."

"How did the raid turn out?"

"Fourteen dead. Six cops and agents, and eight gang members."

"You saved her." She trailed a line of kisses down his jaw. "I bet your sister was so thankful for what you did for her."

"Actually, she was pretty angry with me for dragging her away from … wait, did you say my sister?"

When they'd been dating, she had met Jett's mother, his two brothers, and three of his sisters. But there was a fourth sister that he never really talked about, and Savannah had assumed she was the one who had gotten messed up in drugs and gangs. "She was who you saved, right?"

"She wasn't my sister. She was a friend."

Savannah pulled away from Jett, out of his embrace. "A friend?" she echoed.

"We grew up together, went to school together," Jett elaborated.

"So, you were just friends?" she asked, not sure she wanted to know the answer. How would she feel if instead of being there to support her when she had to testify against the man who had nearly killed her, he had been off rescuing an old girlfriend?

Jett looked away, no longer meeting her gaze squarely, and she had her answer.

Still, she needed to hear him admit it. "Jett? Were you more than just friends with her?"

He sighed. "We were childhood sweethearts," he admitted. "But it was over a long time ago, Savannah. When she chose drugs and then the gang over me, it was over."

So, he hadn't even been the one to end things.

"I just couldn't let her die. That was it. Nothing more. I wanted to be with you when you testified, more than anything, but I couldn't have lived with myself if she died, and I could have done something to stop it."

He had chosen an old girlfriend over her. How was she ever going to trust him to be there in the future?

The short answer was, she couldn't.

Whatever might have been able to be salvaged and repaired between them was over.

* * * * *

7:18 P.M.

Sawyer Watson hoped that his sister and Jett Crane were able to sort things out between them.

Sometimes he really didn't get how his twin's mind worked. Savannah still loved Jett. Okay, so she was hurt about some choices he'd made, that was fine, be mad, but then get over it. If you had love—real, true, storybook, fairy-tale, happily ever after love—then why would you let it go for anything?

He would give pretty much anything to have the woman of his dreams.

Ashley Fallon.

Five-foot three. Long, jet-black hair. Dark brown eyes that you lost yourself in when you stared into their bottomless depths. Milky white skin that he was positive felt as soft as it looked. And the perfect body, curves in all the right places. She was the smartest and funniest person he knew. She was also the sweetest and the most hardworking.

She was perfection.

Unfortunately for him, it was never going to happen. He and Ashley were firmly in the friend zone, and if it came down to keeping her as a friend, or asking her out and losing her, then he was going to have to find a way to be content as friends because there was no way he was going to lose her.

His sister really didn't know how lucky she had it that the man she loved actually loved her back. If she didn't get that, then he was going to have to sit her down and make her see it. Savannah had been through a lot, and she deserved some happiness, even if she didn't think so.

Sometimes Savannah was her own worst enemy.

He'd give it another hour or so, and if he hadn't heard from Savannah, he would assume things had gone well and head over to spend the night in his car watching over Jett's house. It wasn't that he didn't trust the FBI agent to keep his sister safe; it was just that this was his sister, and he wasn't taking any chances.

When he heard from Savannah depended on how she reacted to what Jett told her. Sawyer already knew the reason why Jett hadn't been with Savannah when she testified in court. His sister may not have been prepared to hear him out, but he had been. He'd wanted to know why Jett had hurt Savannah, and once he'd heard what he'd been doing, he'd understood. Sometimes you got caught between two people you cared about, and there was no good choice to make because whatever you ended up doing, someone would get hurt. Unfortunately, this time, the one who had been hurt was Savannah, but if Jett had stayed with her, then Amanda Billow could be dead right now. He really hoped his sister could set aside her hurt and any potential jealousy and just let herself be happy.

He hoped it was a good sign that he hadn't heard from Savannah yet. If he knew his twin sister, she would first want to know why Jett hadn't been there while she'd been testifying before she let herself entertain the possibility of a reconciliation.

Even if she did understand why Jett had felt like he had to go and help save his ex-girlfriend, that didn't mean she would be ready to restart their relationship. Sawyer believed she would, but Savannah was a whole lot more cautious than he was. If it was him, he would be wanting to make up for lost time, but Savannah might want to come back here later. Either way, he would be watching over her.

He and Savannah didn't have any other family left. Their dad had died when they were nine, their mom not long after their twenty-first birthdays. They didn't have any other siblings, so since it was just the two of them, they looked out for each other. He'd been there for her every step of the way during her recoveries from both attacks, although he had taken a step back and let Jett take over when Savannah had started dating him.

Now, more than ever, he needed the distraction of taking care of his sister. Anything to get him out of the office. Being stuck there day in and day out with Ashley, watching her date, sitting beside her every day. Being unable to touch her was torture, when all he wanted to do was wrap a fist around her long black hair, pull her head back until that slim white neck was exposed, then trail a line of kisses all the way from those plump pink lips, down her slender neck, paying special attention to her round breasts, across her flat stomach, before settling between her—

His phone buzzed in his pocket, and he pulled it out. Savannah's name flashed on the screen. That couldn't be good. Sawyer guessed Jett's explanation didn't go down well. He pressed answer, and before he could even say hello, his sister started to speak.

"Sawyer, can you come and get me? Now."

"Don't you think you and Jett should talk?" He didn't want to see Savannah ruin the best thing that'd ever happened to her just because her feelings were hurt.

"I think we've talked more than enough." Savannah sounded like she was crying, and the urge to pummel Jett for making his sister cry surged through him, even if he did understand the position Jett had been in.

"Sav, listen to him. What choice did he have?"

"You knew?" she asked quietly. Whenever she was upset, Savannah always grew quiet.

"Just because you chose not to listen to Jett doesn't mean I had to go the same route."

"Why didn't you tell me?"

"Because I believe your exact words were, 'I don't want to hear anything Jett Crane has to say.'"

"Whatever," she muttered. "Will you please just come and get me?"

Sawyer was tempted to say no, so she'd be stranded there with no choice but to talk to Jett and sort things out. But knowing Savannah, she would find a way to get home herself, and with a dangerous ex-FBI agent threatening her, he didn't want to leave her alone and unprotected. "Okay. I'll be there in ten."

"You don't know where I am."

He knew exactly where she was. He had helped Jett set everything up, including driving around to a dozen bakeries to find all the things his sister usually baked at Christmas. "You're at Jett's."

"Right," she mumbled under her breath. "You helped him plan this. Fine. Ten minutes. I'll be waiting outside."

"You can't, Sav," he reminded her. "You can't be on your own until we find Blake. Wait inside until I get there."

"Jett said there are agents watching his house; I'll be fine."

There was no point arguing with his stubborn sister, so Sawyer disconnected the call, grabbed his keys, and jumped in his car. He'd go and pick up Savannah, bring her home, and let her digest what she had learned tonight. But this wasn't the end. If he couldn't have the woman he wanted, then he was going to make darn sure that Savannah got the man she wanted, even if she kept forgetting that she wanted him. At least one of them deserved to be happy.

* * * * *

10:41 P.M.

He had been so close.

Jett really thought that he and Savannah had a chance at fixing things between them and getting back together.

But now, he wasn't so sure.

He wasn't giving up, but he couldn't force Savannah to change her mind either. If she decided that she didn't love him anymore and didn't want them to be together, then there was nothing he could do about it. But if she thought she got to walk away tonight and shut him out, she had another thing coming.

He'd give her tonight. That was fair enough, but she wouldn't get any longer. She'd been understanding about why he hadn't been there for her that day; she was just stuck on the person whose life he'd been saving was his childhood sweetheart.

Amanda Billow and her family had grown up around the block from his. They went to the same school—all the way from preschool to high school. When they were five, he'd asked her to marry him, and they had a make-believe wedding in her backyard with all their friends. When they were ten, they'd shared their first kiss behind the school's gym. When they were twelve, they went on their first date to a school dance. Even then, he'd thought he and Amanda were in love and that they would grow up together and get married for real and start a family of their own.

Then everything had changed.

Jett's dad left, and his responsibilities at home took over his life. He barely had time to get his schoolwork done between taking care of things at home, let alone continue to play football and hang out with his girlfriend.

Still, they tried to keep things going. Sometimes Amanda would come home with him after school and help do chores or play with his younger siblings.

But then, Amanda's family blew up too.

Her parents got divorced, and when neither wanted full custody, she and her sister were bounced back and forth between the two. Amanda made it okay through that first year, but then when her older sister went off to college and she was left all alone, things started to fall apart.

Despite neither parent wanting to be stuck with their kids, they were awarded joint legal and physical custody. With her dad going through a midlife crisis and obsessing over various pursuits from running marathons to climbing Mount Everest, and her mother going through her own midlife crisis and becoming obsessed with plastic surgery and finding rich boyfriends to fund it, Amanda felt lost and alone.

That was when she turned to drugs.

Jett had seen her starting to slip away, not just from him, but from the girl she used to be, and, in the end, he had given her an ultimatum. Him or the drugs. Amanda had chosen the drugs.

By the time she turned sixteen, she was nothing like the girl he had grown up with.

She dropped out of school, started prostituting herself to gang members for drugs, then she started dealing, and when she started sleeping with one of the gang leaders, Jett knew that Amanda was truly gone.

Although he'd never completely forgotten about her, he had moved on with his life. Graduated high school, gone on to college, joined the FBI, met Savannah, and fallen in love. Amanda had just become part of his past.

Until he'd gotten that call.

There was no way he could let her get killed in the shootout with the cops he knew would come. So, he'd dropped everything and gone to rescue her. Maybe he shouldn't have, or maybe he should have, all he knew was he wasn't the kind of guy who stood by and watched someone get hurt. If someone he cared about needed him, then he was there. And at one point in his life, he had loved Amanda. It wasn't the same kind of love he felt for Savannah, and it never would have been, but she'd been his childhood sweetheart, and she was special to him.

If he was honest, it hurt that Savannah had shut him out so completely without even giving him an opportunity to explain. That wasn't what you did when you were in love with someone. You gave them the benefit of the doubt.

Although it hurt, it wasn't something Jett would hold against her. Just like his past had shaped him into the man he was, the man who couldn't abandon someone who meant something to him, it had done the same to Savannah. And at that time in her life, asking her to understand why he hadn't stood by her side while she'd faced the monster who'd almost stolen her life had been too much.

But that was nearly three years ago.

She didn't get to keep using that as an excuse.

She loved him. She even wanted to forgive him and try to find a way to get back what they'd had before. He knew that. The way she melted every time he spoke to her, how she stared at him longingly, the way her body trembled every time he touched her.

He had to believe that she could accept that doing what he had to do to save Amanda's life didn't mean that she was a threat to their relationship. He didn't love Amanda, and she certainly didn't love him. She'd been furious that he'd dragged her away from the man she believed she loved and pulled strings to have her put in a rehab facility.

There was not now and never would be a future for him and Amanda.

He and Savannah, on the other hand—he really hoped they had one.

He'd fight for her, but in the end, if she couldn't accept his need to help those who needed it, then she didn't really understand him. And if she didn't really understand who he was, then it didn't matter that they loved each other; they would never work as a couple.

That was something he wasn't ready to consider yet.

He had to believe that in time, she would let go of this jealousy.

In a way, it was kind of a compliment that she loved him so much, even the thought of him putting another woman above her hurt like crazy.

Right now, as much as he wanted to sit Savannah down and make her understand, he had to keep his focus on Blake.

Just like he had every other time, his ex-partner had been well enough prepared to escape eight highly trained and prepared FBI agents.

Blake must have had a car hidden someplace on the other side of the river. Jett had thought he'd gotten them when he shot at the boat and made it sink. He'd thought it would buy him and Tom and the others enough time to get over there and arrest him.

But, once again, they'd been too slow, and now Blake had more cause than ever to go after Savannah.

He hadn't done what Blake wanted.

Instead of leaving him and Violet alone, he'd tried once again to stop him.

Jett knew what that meant.

Blake was coming.

It was only a matter of time.

He would come for Savannah.

When he'd told Savannah about Amanda, she'd shut down as soon as she learned that he and Amanda had dated. She'd called her brother, then insisted on waiting outside for Sawyer to arrive. He'd let her only because there were enough agents watching his house to keep her safe if Blake showed up. That and he'd stood at his front window, gun in hand, watching her like a hawk until Sawyer's car pulled to a stop outside his house.

He'd intended to let her have tonight, then go and see her tomorrow and try explaining to her again that Amanda meant nothing to him other than a person from his past whose well-being he still cared about. He just wasn't sure he could leave her alone tonight. Jett knew Sawyer was with her, and there were half a dozen agents, plus a couple of local cops, watching her house, but it didn't seem like enough. Locking her down inside a safehouse or a police station didn't seem like enough. Locking her down in the middle of the FBI building didn't seem like enough. Removing her from the planet didn't seem like enough.

Blake was too dangerous, and he wouldn't stop until he got his revenge.

That was it.

He was spending the night on Savannah's couch.

Maybe that would help to alleviate his fears.

Only, Jett knew it wouldn't. The only thing that was going to alleviate his fears was standing over his ex-partner's dead body.

He hadn't wanted it to end that way, but no one threatened the woman he loved and got away with it. There were only two ways this would end—either with his and Savannah's deaths or with Blake's. And he had no intention of dying.

DECEMBER 23RD

12:05 A.M.

"She's not going to be pleased you're here."

"I'm sure she's not," Jett agreed as Sawyer let him into Savannah's house. Right now, he didn't care if she was happy to see him or not. He was going to be here to protect her when Blake came for her; she was just going to have to deal with that.

"You didn't have to come—there are enough of us here watching over her," Sawyer said as he locked the door and reset the alarm.

"I couldn't be anywhere else," he said quietly. Nothing would have stopped him from being here for her tonight. Nothing.

"Yeah." Sawyer nodded, and from the look on his face, he understood. Jett wondered who he was in love with.

"Where is she?" He knew that Savannah wasn't going to be thrilled that he was here, but he needed to see her. She didn't realize yet just how dangerous Blake really was. She still remembered the kind, compassionate, dedicated FBI agent she had first met four years ago when she was injured and groggy and lying in a hospital bed. But Blake wasn't that man anymore. Blake would slaughter her for no other reason than because he wanted to hurt Jett. And he wouldn't be quick about it. He would make sure she suffered first.

"She's in the attic."

"The attic?" He'd thought she would be in bed getting some sleep. Did she forget she was suffering from a concussion? "What's she doing up there?"

"I don't know. She asked me to help her up there when we got

111

back here."

Intrigued, Jett left Sawyer in the living room and headed to the hallway where the pulldown stairs to the attic were. He climbed them quietly, not wanting to startle her. They were all on edge right now, and the last thing she needed was for him to sneak up on her and scare her.

When he reached the attic, he found her sitting in a corner in her wheelchair with a large book opened on her lap. As he walked closer, he saw it was a photo album, and he immediately knew what she was looking at.

Jett was about to announce his presence when she spoke. "I knew you'd come. You can never stay away when someone needs saving."

Said the pot to the kettle, he thought to himself.

In some ways, he and Savannah were very much alike. Growing up with so many responsibilities resting on his shoulders had embedded in him a need to always do the right thing and help anyone around him who needed it. And what had happened to Savannah when she was a kid had instilled in her a need to save anyone who was in trouble. It had led to her first assault and to her getting mixed up in this case. If she had just called 911 like a normal person instead of running straight toward trouble, she never would have wound up on Blake's radar.

"How can I stay away from you?" he asked, taking a step closer.

With her gaze still fixed firmly on the photos in her lap, she said, "I'm sorry, Jett. I know I'm being ridiculously unfair to you. I get it; I do. I get why you went to save her. It was her life at stake. With my situation, it was just that I needed some moral support to face my personal monster. But I did it. I did it without you. And if you'd told me what you needed to do, I would have told you to go. I know I should be fine with this, and I wish I was. But I can't help it. I'm hurt, and I'm …"

Jealous.

That was how he hoped she'd been intending to finish that sentence.

"It's okay, Savannah," he assured her.

"I'm being stupid and selfish. I know that. I love that you're the kind of guy who is always there when someone needs you, who would risk anything to help someone. I'm sorry," she finished helplessly, finally looking up at him.

"Don't be sorry for your feelings, but you have to understand that there hasn't been anything between me and Amanda for a long time."

"Amanda? That's her name?"

"Amanda Billow."

"Where is she now?"

"Last I heard she was back in prison."

"She wasn't even grateful for what you did for her?"

"No, she wasn't. But I didn't do it for her thanks. I did it because it was the right thing to do because she deserved a chance to decide how the rest of her life would play out. And given the choice again, I'd still make the same one." Jett waited anxiously to see her response to that. He wasn't used to this feeling of uneasiness. He hated feeling like this; he was used to being in control. Only Savannah could make him feel this out of his element.

Instead of getting angry, or worse, upset, Savannah actually smiled at him. "I know you would because you're a good guy."

He didn't smile back at her. She might not have said it, but he knew what she was thinking. That she wasn't good. That couldn't be more wrong. He crossed the rest of the way over to her and stood in front of her. "One day, you're going to have to accept that what happened wasn't your fault. There was nothing else you could do. You have to stop punishing yourself."

She said nothing, just shifted her gaze back to the photos.

"Savannah," he said, feeling even more helpless, and dropped to his knees beside her wheelchair. "You have to let it go."

"Let it go?" she echoed. "How can I do that?"

"Because holding on to it is killing you."

"He died, Jett. *Died.*" A tear rolled down her cheek, followed by another and another.

He reached out and caught them with the pads of his thumbs, brushing them away. "I know he did, sweetheart." If he could take that pain away, he would in a heartbeat. He'd take it and make it his own, so she could finally be free.

"It doesn't matter what I do; it's never enough. It's never enough to make up for not saving him." Helplessness fell with each tear, and he wished she could cry it right out of her soul.

"He wouldn't want you to blame yourself."

"You never even met him," she reminded him.

"He made you. I know what kind of man your father was, and I know that he would hate to see you beating yourself up over what happened. I'm not just saying this to make you feel better, Savannah. It really was not your fault." Jett wanted to order her to believe that.

"You shouldn't be so nice to me. Not after the way I treated you. I should have let you explain back then, and tonight I shouldn't have run away scared."

"What are you scared of, Sav?" If he could get to the bottom of her fears, then maybe he could find a way to help her overcome them. Once she found a way to let them go, maybe they could finally be happy together.

She stared at the album in her lap for another moment before slowly lifting her eyes to meet his. So many emotions bubbled inside those big blue eyes, but it was the trust that punched him in the gut.

Savannah trusted him.

Despite him abandoning her when she needed him the most— even if it was for a good cause—and her declarations that she could never trust him again, she did.

She believed that he could help her find a way to move

forward, even if moving forward terrified her more than anything else.

The only thing holding her back was fear.

He was about to reassure her that there was nothing they couldn't handle together when he heard a thump downstairs. From the way her head darted toward the top of the stairs as she stretched out a hand to seek out his, Savannah had heard it too.

Blake couldn't really make it in here, could he?

There were eight law enforcement officials watching the house, plus Sawyer downstairs.

Yes, he had needed to be here tonight, but it wasn't because he truly thought Blake would try anything; it was just because not having Savannah where he could see her terrified him.

"Go hide in the corner," he whispered. He should never have allowed himself to get distracted. He knew better. Keeping Savannah alive should have been the only thing he cared about.

"Jett," she whispered back, her scared eyes finding his, pleading with him not to leave her. But if Blake was really here in her house, Jett wanted her safely tucked away.

"Now," he hissed back, harsher than he intended, but his heart was drumming in his chest as fear flowed through his veins. "Don't come out, no matter what happens."

Reluctantly, she withdrew her hand to put them on the wheelchair's wheels and began to head for the farthest corner of the attic.

Jett pulled out his gun and headed for the stairs. If Blake had found his way into Savannah's house, then he wasn't making it out of it alive.

* * * * *

12:27 A.M.

She was terrified.

Usually, when Savannah found herself in a dangerous situation, it was because she had gone running straight toward it. She never had time to really think about what she was doing or to dwell on it; she just acted on instinct. But now, someone was in her home in the middle of the night.

Someone who wanted to kill her.

As she wheeled toward the corner, Jett headed for the stairs. She wanted to grab hold of him and beg him to stay with her, to be safe, to not get himself killed. Although it was hard for her to picture the FBI agent who had worked her case as a violent monster, she knew that's what he was. Savannah understood how dangerous he was and how much of a threat he presented—not just to her but to Jett too.

"Be careful, please," she whispered under her breath as he took the first step down the stairs. She didn't know how she would cope if anything happened to Jett. Things between them may still be messed up, but she couldn't deny that she still loved him and that she wanted to work things out.

If Blake Sedenker was here and he got his hands on Jett, he'd kill him. If he was here in her house, he might have already killed her brother.

Sawyer.

If he died because of her, just like her father had, she would never forgive herself. Her brother was the only family she had left, and they'd always been close. She couldn't lose him.

Jett and Sawyer were the two men she loved most in the world. She couldn't let Jett go down there alone. She'd already distracted him with her reminiscing to the point that he'd forgotten that he was supposed to be on guard. She had to go with him. If he had his backup weapon on him, he could give it to her, and she could cover his back.

He was just disappearing down another step when the room was suddenly plunged into darkness.

No, not just the room, the entire house.

"Jett." She started to roll toward him.

"Stay there," he hissed, going down another step.

His head was just disappearing from view when he was suddenly slammed backward.

Blake really was here.

What should she do?

She wanted to do things the smart way this time and not the impulsive way she usually rushed into things. If she messed this up, then they would all wind up dead. Her gun was in its lockbox down in the hall closet, and there was no way to get to it since Blake was there. She didn't have her phone on her either. When Sawyer had brought her home, she asked him to bring her straight up here, leaving her bag—with her cell inside it—on the table by the front door. Savannah had known she was being unfair to Jett with her reactions to what he'd told her, and she needed to do some soul-searching to find a way to be okay, to be normal.

A rolling ball of limbs suddenly crashed across the attic floor.

That was it.

She wasn't sitting here hiding while Jett fought for both their lives.

Frantically, her eyes searched the dark attic for anything she could use to fight Blake with.

Think, think, think.

There had to be something here she could use as a weapon.

Something.

Anything.

She tried to run through in her mind exactly what was up here. It was mostly keepsakes from her childhood and things from her mom's house that she hadn't been able to part with after she died. There were the empty boxes where she stored her Christmas decorations and her old kayaking things.

There was a paddle with her kayaking things.

She hadn't used them since well before her first accident, but she'd kept them, unable to get rid of them because they represented freedom from her past that she feared she could never get back. She used to love taking her kayak out early in the mornings to a quiet, peaceful lake. She'd paddle around, watching the sun rise, listening to a chorus of bird chirps, a mist floating atop the water fading away as the world woke up. That used to be the one time she actually felt at peace.

Now it might be the one thing that saved their lives.

Where was it?

Savannah couldn't remember. She wasn't a really organized person, and organizing the attic had never seemed worth her time.

She looked over at where the men were wrestling on the floor. Jett was on top, his fists pummeling Blake's face.

Maybe everything would be okay anyway.

Jett was so big and so strong, there was no way Blake could win against him.

Just as Savannah was relaxing, Blake suddenly managed to lunge up off the floor, tackling Jett backward and sending them both crashing into a pile of boxes.

She couldn't let Jett do this alone.

He thought that she was just going to do as he said and hide, but he had to know by now that wasn't who she was.

Even though it was dark, she closed her eyes to concentrate.

The kayaking things were over in the corner behind the Christmas boxes. She'd almost rolled over a paddle when Chloe and Fin were helping her get her decorations and sort out which of her Christmas trees she would put up this year. She had a bit of a Christmas tree addiction and owned six in various sizes—plus, she sometimes opted for a real tree.

The Christmas boxes were in the adjacent corner.

Knowing she would need the element of surprise on her side to do anything effective to help Jett, Savannah did her best not to draw attention to herself. There were two of them to Blake's one, so they should be able to take him. Once they got him under control, they could cuff him, arrest him, and drag him off to prison where he belonged.

Luck was on her side, and the paddles were leaning up against the boxes instead of lying on the floor where it would have been difficult for her to reach.

Before she had time to think about what she was doing, she wheeled herself as hard as she could toward the wrestling men, swinging the paddle with as much precision as she could in the dark. Somehow, she managed to connect with Blake's head.

He grunted in surprise and shoved her backward.

She was too close to the stairs.

Savannah didn't have time to gain control of her wheelchair.

Just like the other night, Blake sent her skidding backward; only this time, instead of connecting with the gatepost, she went careening down the steps.

Each bump caused new bruises on top of her old ones.

The world spun around her, and she lost her sense of direction as she rolled over and over and over before landing with a thud that pushed the air from her lungs.

Voices swirled around her.

Footsteps too.

Then the sound of breaking glass.

A body knelt beside her, and she shrank away from it, afraid it was Blake.

Between the lights being out and the fall, she couldn't see or hear properly, but when hands lightly touched her neck, she relaxed.

She knew that touch.

It was Jett.

More voices joined the cacophony of loud noises swarming around her head. Some part of her knew it was just the agents who were watching the house roused by the scuffle, but she still shied away from them.

Light flooded over her, and her eyes immediately scrunched closed against the pain that stabbed at her eyeballs.

Where was Blake?

She had to know where he was.

"B-Blake?" she tried to ask, but it came out as a hoarse croak.

"Don't try to talk," Jett said, his voice close and comforting.

When he scooped her up into his arms, she clung to him. She wasn't letting him go—not ever again. Whatever drama she had created between them by being selfish was over and done with. She wanted Jett if he would have her.

"How badly are you hurt?" he asked as he laid her down on what she assumed was her couch.

"I-I don't think I'm hurt. Just sore," she replied. While her body ached with a dull thudding pain, there was no one place that drew her attention, so she didn't think anything was broken. "Where's Blake?"

Unfortunately, he didn't give her the answer she wanted to hear. "He got away." Jett's voice was grim as his fingers brushed lightly across her forehead. He tucked her hair behind her ears, his fingertips lingering on her skin, making it tingle beneath his touch.

Savannah forced her eyelids open, squinting at the still-too-bright light. If Blake got away, it meant that Jett wouldn't be able to stay, that he would have to go looking for him. Right now, she was selfish enough to want him—need him—by her side. Surely, he could spare just a couple of hours to hold her while she slept.

She was about to ask him to stay when she suddenly darted straight up.

Sawyer.

Where was her twin?

Moving too quickly had been a bad idea.

The world faded in and out of focus.

She heard Jett speak, maybe something about getting her a doctor, but she couldn't make out the words.

Pain knifed through her skull, reminding her she was still suffering from a concussion.

This second bump to her head, even if it was a minor one,

couldn't be good.

Savannah fought against it, but unconsciousness wrapped its dark tentacles around her and dragged her under.

* * * * *

12:42 A.M.

"Savannah?"

A second ago, she had been awake and talking, but now her eyes rolled back in her head, and she slumped backward.

Jett caught her as she fell and eased her back to lie against the pillows.

For a second, he just stared at her, dumbfounded, his brain trying to convince him that she was dead.

But she wasn't dead.

Her skin was warm beneath his hand. Her chest rose and fell evenly with each breath she took, and her pulse fluttered in the hollow of her neck.

Savannah was alive.

She'd just fainted.

"I need a doctor here. Now," he yelled to no one in particular.

"Paramedics are on the way. What happened here?" Tom Drake asked, appearing beside him.

"What do you think? Blake Sedenker. He tried to make good on his threat to kill Savannah if I didn't stay away from him and Violet."

If Blake had succeeded, it would have been his fault.

He knew better than to get distracted when he was working such a dangerous case.

Savannah was his top priority. And as much as he was dying to rekindle what they'd had, he was going to have to find a balance between that and keeping her safe.

"Ugh," Savannah groaned and groggily opened her eyes.

"Don't try to sit up," he ordered, mostly to release some of the anxiety churning in his gut.

She ignored him and tried to push herself up. Jett thought about putting his hands on her shoulders and holding her down, but he'd rather hold her, so instead, he lifted her legs and sat beside her, then he slid her onto his lap.

"Where's Sawyer?" she asked, looking around in a panic.

"Right here," her brother said, leaning on the back of the couch.

"Are you okay?"

"I'm fine; Blake just tased me."

"And now he's gone again." Her blue eyes met Jett's, and something flitted through them. There was the pain she was no doubt feeling, and the fear that came from the man who wanted to kill her still being on the loose, but there was something else there too.

"I'll find him," he assured her, even though he was starting to doubt that was the case. Blake was too smart, too prepared, and too obsessed.

Savannah sank down against him, nestling her head on his shoulder. "Just don't get yourself killed. Please."

So, that's what was bothering her. She was afraid. For him. That gave him a high he hadn't experienced in a long time. He was used to getting highs from hunting killers, but he hadn't dated since he and Savannah broke up, and he missed having someone care about him that way.

"I wish you could stay here with me for a while," she continued, lightly kissing his neck in the exact spot behind his ear that she knew got to him the same way it got to her. "I know it's selfish."

"You are the least selfish person I know," he told her, turning his head so he could kiss her forehead. "And you don't have to worry about me. I won't let anything stop me from coming home to you."

She shuddered in his arms, and he hoped it was a good shudder. He hoped it meant that she wanted to come home each night to him too.

Ignoring her brother and Tom and the other agents buzzing about the house, he took hold of her chin and angled her face up so he could kiss her properly. No more chaste kisses on the forehead or teasing kisses on the neck—he was done with that.

Now he wanted a real kiss.

One where he could taste her, one that left them both breathless and wanting more.

When he finally took her mouth, it was like their first kiss all over again.

He curled a hand around the back of her head, tangling his fingers in her hair and brought her closer. Not to be left out, Savannah wrapped her arms around his neck and angled her head to give him better access.

His tongue darted inside her mouth, reminding him of another part of her body he wanted to enter, and she moaned against him, pressing closer still until she was all but plastered across his chest.

Without him even realizing it, one hand traced a line from her neck down between her breasts and settled on her stomach. Savannah let her own hands trail from his neck down to his chest.

Jett slipped his hands under the hem of her sweatshirt and was ready to set everything else aside to whisk her away to her bedroom where they could spend some time—just the two of them—reconnecting and getting reacquainted with each other's bodies.

"Ahem." Someone cleared their throat nearby.

With a groan, Jett broke the kiss, his heavy breathing echoing Savannah's, and with great difficulty, he was able to tear his gaze from hers.

"Paramedics are here," Tom announced.

Right.

Paramedics.

Because Savannah was hurt, and he was mauling her like a starving teenager.

"I don't really need a doctor," Savannah protested, still staring longingly at him.

"You need to be checked out. Please, Savannah, I need to know you're okay," he added when she got that determined look in her eyes that said she was going to go and get all stubborn and refuse to be examined.

She smiled and gave a small laugh. He loved that sound. He could listen to it forever and never tire of hearing it. "Okay, if it's that important to you, I'll go with the nice medic and let him check me out."

Because he knew it was what was best for her, Jett slowly slid her off his lap and stood so the middle-aged medic could get to her.

"Don't worry," the man grinned at him. "I'll take just as good care of your girl as if she were my girl."

His girl.

Jett liked the sound of that.

And by the goofy, lovestruck smile she had on her face, Savannah did too.

"Jett."

He wanted to ignore Tom, live in this moment a little longer, let his responsibilities go for just one minute. Surely there was nothing wrong with that. He deserved just a few minutes to worry about his girlfriend—at least, he hoped they were dating again. As far as he was concerned, they were—and think about what he'd do to her when he got her alone and in bed.

"We have to figure out where Blake Sedenker is before he comes back to finish what he started tonight."

Jett sighed.

Break time was over.

"How did he get in here?" he asked.

"From what we can figure, somehow he got the names of the

people watching Savannah's house. He came to the door disguised as one of them—"

"A woman," Sawyer inserted. "He looked like a woman. I checked the identification, it looked legitimate. If it didn't, I would never have let him in."

Sawyer looked guilty enough without him adding to it.

"She asked to use the bathroom," Sawyer continued. "I said yes. I've done stakeouts before, I know how bad it can get. As soon as I closed the door behind him, he tased me."

"It wasn't your fault, Sawyer. I lost my focus, as well." It couldn't happen again though. He was going to have to find a balance between his job and his relationship.

"Where would he go next? What would he do?" Tom asked. "You know him better than anyone else, Jett. He's lost the old bed and breakfast, and he still has Violet. What would his next move be?"

He pondered that for a moment.

For Blake, it wasn't just about being obsessed with Violet Fisher. It went deeper than that. He wanted to recreate something with her, something that he felt he had lost with his ex-wife.

Blake wanted a family.

That was why he had killed Violet's family instead of just abducting her. He didn't want her to have any ties to her old life because he wanted to create a new one with her.

With her and his daughter.

"Laila."

"His daughter. You think he's going to try and grab her?"

"He knows he can't hang around here forever. If he does, then sooner or later he's going to get caught. His best bet at evading us long-term is to get as far away as he can, but he's not going to go without his daughter. He has Violet now, he took her to a place where he thought the relationship he believes they have could grow, so the next logical step would be to get his daughter back. We have to get to Georgette's house."

"You don't look like you should be going anywhere right now." Tom gestured to his face, and Jett lifted a hand and touched his cheek, surprised when his fingers came away sticky with blood.

"I'm fine," he said, satisfied to know he got in as many good hits to Blake as his ex-partner had gotten in on him.

"No," Tom said firmly. "You made Savannah get checked out; you need to as well. Let the medics check you out, then we can head to Blake's ex-wife's house. I'll call the agents watching it and make sure they're aware that we think he might be ready to make his move."

Jett hated to admit it, but Tom was right. If he was hurt, then he wasn't in any condition to take on Blake.

And now more than ever, he had a reason to come home safe.

* * * * *

2:17 A.M.

Even though things hadn't gone as planned tonight, Blake was feeling good. Happy, even. It had been a long time since he'd felt anything other than crushing rage.

Rage had been his life for a long time.

Since he was a child.

His ex-partner thought that it was Martha Hobbs, the woman who had sold her four young daughters, that had changed him, but Jett was wrong. He'd always been messed up inside; he just used to be better at hiding it.

Blake knew how Martha's children felt growing up with such a despicable excuse for a human being as a mother.

He knew because his mother had also been a despicable human being.

He had never known his father. He wasn't even sure his mother knew who he was since there was no father listed on his birth certificate, and she had never mentioned him. Besides, if she'd known who he was, she probably would have tried to palm him off on him since being stuck with a child was the last thing she wanted.

Blake knew that because she'd told him often when he was growing up.

His mother was a successful businesswoman who owned and ran a chain of spas. He'd always thought that was ironic that she was in the beauty industry, obsessed with looking younger as she aged, and yet she was a truly ugly person inside and out.

Tiana Sedenker was a cruel woman.

Besides her job, the only thing in the world that she seemed to enjoy was thinking up new and inventive ways to punish him.

When he was three, her favorite thing to do was lock him in the closet because he was afraid of the dark. She'd leave him there until he'd wet himself and lost his voice from screaming. By the time he was seven, she'd grown bored with that form of torture and had taken to throwing him in the pool and making him stay in there for hours until his skin was painfully pruned. Next came a fascination with bugs. When he was around eleven, she would cut his skin and then put maggots in the wound and let them eat at his flesh. Then he got too big for her to physically punish, so she started trying to deprive him of sleep. She would wait till he drifted off, then wake him up, doing it over and over again until he could count the amount of sleep he got in minutes and walked around for days in a fog.

No one knew what was going on in his house.

To the outside world, he was just a smart but quiet boy who lived a privileged life and had the best of everything that money could buy. But inside, he was seething. All he could think about was hurting his mother. Killing her. Slowly. Making her feel the same pain she had inflicted on him.

In the end, he'd made it quick.

It was too risky.

Especially with his mother having such a high-profile job.

A couple of sleeping pills mixed with too much alcohol had to suffice.

No one had ever thought to investigate. Everyone who knew her knew that she drank—a lot—and that she frequently used sleeping pills, often disregarding the dangers and mixing the two. Her death was deemed an accident.

No one knew the truth.

Only him.

She deserved what she got, and all he wished was that he'd been able to make her suffer.

Aged sixteen when his mother died, he became an emancipated minor and started working while completing high school. Blake had worked as hard as he could to achieve his dream job. The chance to get the justice he never did, to take down criminals.

Sometimes even to shoot them.

With each case he worked, it got harder and harder to keep the beast that lived inside him quiet.

It wanted to break out.

It wanted to hurt others.

The evilness he had inherited from his mother wanted to take over, but his father must have been a good man, and that goodness lived inside him too.

A constant battle.

Good versus evil.

Except when it came to his daughter.

He had never laid a hand on Laila.

He'd been a good, loving, and nurturing father, despite all the odds of his upbringing and his chosen career. He'd been warm and sensitive when it came to his little girl.

Georgette had no right to take his child away from him.

. She was no better than his mother had been. Ripping a child away from her father was just another form of child abuse.

And just like his mother, she would be punished.

Martha Hobbs and her children hadn't been the catalyst for this; they had just been the key that finally unlocked the door that kept the monster locked away.

He couldn't hold it back any longer.

He hadn't wanted to.

He was tired of letting evil go unpunished.

So instead of going home to his family each night, he'd started stalking the ones who'd gotten away. The cases they hadn't had enough evidence to convict, or the ones who had hired fancy defense lawyers to get them off on technicalities.

This was his true calling.

Hunting criminals.

After Laila, it was the single most important thing in his life.

Only Georgette hadn't understood. She hadn't understood that the alcohol was the only thing that helped to keep old memories at bay. She hadn't understood that his life wasn't spinning out of control; it was finally spinning *into* control.

She had walked away, taking his daughter with her.

And the only person who cared was Violet.

Violet was the other piece of his heart, the one he'd thought he would never find. Now he had her with him; the only thing missing was Laila.

Not for much longer.

He slowed the car as he passed the house, then leaned over and opened the passenger door, pushing a tied-up Violet out.

The car wasn't going fast enough to cause her any real harm, and she would be the perfect distraction.

As he drove off around the block, he checked in his rear vision mirror and was smugly pleased to see the two agents who were watching Georgette's house jump out of their sedan and run to Violet.

Blake pulled his car over to the side of the road and jumped out, quietly circling back around until he was behind the FBI agents. While they were preoccupied with untying Violet and tending to any minor wounds she may have sustained, he fired two shots, one into the back of each of their heads.

Both agents dropped immediately.

His silencer muffled the sounds of the gunshots, but they still made a nice popping sound.

He liked the way their heads snapped forward, and their bodies slumped over. He probably shouldn't enjoy it so much. These men weren't bad, and they had been his colleagues only a year ago, but they were hunting him, and that put them on opposing teams.

With no time to spare, he grabbed Violet, who had a few scratches, and he was sure some bruises that would show up by morning. Pulling the spare rope from his pocket, he retied her wrists and ankles, then slung her over his shoulder and carried her to the car he had parked in the driveway of the house across the street. The residents were away for Christmas, so he had been able to park it there without it standing out to anyone.

Blake tossed Violet in the trunk then went to deal with the agents' bodies. He wasn't worried that they were still alive. He always hit his target. Dragging the two bodies off the road, he dumped them in the front yard behind the row of trees along the perimeter where they wouldn't be spotted right away. He wanted them to be found, but not until he was ready.

With Violet tucked safely away and the bodies of the dead agents lying on the grass behind him, Blake stood and looked at the house.

They thought they could hide his ex-wife and daughter away, and he wouldn't be able to find them.

They were wrong.

He'd always known where they were—and he always would, thanks to the small tracking implant he had put in his daughter's back when she was a baby, so that if anything ever happened to her, he would be able to find her. He'd always known there were monsters in this world, and he would never allow her to fall into their hands—even if that person was her mother.

Well, Laila had a new mother now.

He, Violet, and Laila—they were a family.

Just the three of them.

They would go away where nobody knew them, where nobody would bother them. Somewhere they would be safe and happy, where Jett Crane wouldn't find him. His ex-partner had meddled in his life enough. Tonight's attempt on Savannah Watson's life had failed, and Blake wasn't sure yet whether he would make another or if Jett had learned his lesson and would finally leave him alone. He still had time to make up his mind what to do with them, but right now, he had other things to take care of.

Using the key he had snagged from one of the agents, he slid it into the lock and opened the front door, stepping inside the house.

It was time to go get his daughter.

* * * * *

3:21 A.M.

He probably shouldn't be feeling this happy.

His ex-partner was still on the loose, and he was a threat to himself, Savannah, Georgette, Laila, Violet, and anyone else who got in his way.

Jett knew all of that, and yet, he was still feeling good, giddy even. Danger had been a part of his life ever since he took on this job, but having Savannah back meant everything to him. It made everything look like roses and rainbows.

He smirked.

Roses and rainbows.

He wasn't a roses and rainbows kind of guy. No one else on the planet other than Savannah could make him think like that.

"What's so funny?" Tom asked.

"Nothing." He wasn't going to ruin his image with girly talk like that. Besides, now wasn't the time to be getting all mushy. He and Tom were on the way to Georgette's house. Communication with the agents watching the house had stopped about fifteen minutes ago. With Blake still on the loose, and his theories that his ex-partner was going to make a play for his daughter, they had been doing regular check-ins. When they got no response on the last one, he and Tom had jumped in the car and were now on their way there.

In his tussle with Blake, he hadn't received more than a few cuts and bruises—nothing serious, and nothing to keep him out of the field. He wasn't going to be sidelined in this case, not for anything. If he had wanted to catch Blake before, that had multiplied by about a million after the man tried to kill Savannah. She was innocent, had nothing to do with this, and she didn't deserve to die just because Blake was angry that Jett wasn't letting him get away.

No matter what Blake did, he would never stop trying to catch him.

Jett knew he would win.

Life wouldn't have reunited him with Savannah only for one or both of them to die at Blake's hand.

As they turned into the street where Georgette and Laila lived, he immediately snapped back into work mode. When he and Savannah finished sorting things out between them, he was going to have to work on not flipping that switch when he was at home. He'd been alone for so long, he was used to work being his life. He ate, slept, and breathed it, often working long into the night and then catching a few hours' sleep before going back into the office. But assuming things with Savannah continued to go well, and they wound up living together and then married, he was going to have to make a change; home would be for home, and work would be for work.

"There's the car," he said, pointing to a black sedan parked across the street from Georgette's.

The car looked empty.

That wasn't a good sign.

They all knew how dangerous Blake Sedenker was, and there was no way those agents would have walked away and left Georgette and Laila unprotected.

Unless they hadn't left by choice.

He and Tom jumped out of the car the second it was parked and ran for the unoccupied sedan.

"He was here," Jett said as he threw open the driver's door.

Without waiting for a response from Tom, he turned and headed for the house. If they were lucky, then Blake might still be in there.

As soon as he passed the trees that bordered the property, he saw them.

Agent Patch and Agent Humphrey lay on the grass.

There was no need to check for a pulse.

They were dead.

Even if he hadn't known that Blake would never leave them alive, he could tell by the awkward way they lay.

"How did he shoot them? They were two highly-trained FBI agents who knew exactly how dangerous Blake is. They wouldn't just let him get close enough to shoot them." Tom knelt and did the obligatory pulse checks.

"He would have used some ploy to distract them," Jett called over his shoulder as he headed for the house. The agents were already dead; there was nothing they could do to help them, but Georgette and Laila may still be alive.

The front door was closed, but when he turned the handle, he found it wasn't locked.

As soon as he stepped inside, he knew.

The metallic smell of blood was thick in the air.

"He killed them," Tom said, joining him in the house.

"Maybe not both of them." Jett believed that Blake wouldn't hurt his daughter. At least, not yet. Right now, Blake wanted her back; he felt that she was his possession, and he wasn't pleased that she'd been taken from him. That wouldn't last, but he wouldn't kill her this quickly.

Guns drawn in case Blake was still here, they headed up the stairs.

Jett had been here before, so he led Tom to Laila's room, bypassing the master bedroom where the smell of blood was even stronger.

The bedroom door was closed, and Tom covered him while he slowly turned the handle and eased it open, half expecting Blake to come bounding out, or start shooting at them, but there was nothing.

Laila wasn't there.

Blake wasn't there.

They were too late.

He had his daughter, and he had Violet; his new little family was complete. There was nothing keeping him here anymore. He would take them both and flee, and they might never find them. Then when Violet or Laila or both of them did something to cross him, he'd kill them too.

As soon as he knew Blake was coming after him by targeting Savannah, he should have known he was almost ready to go after Laila. He should have had them moved, or he should have tried harder to convince Georgette to take her daughter and disappear.

"We have to check out the rest of the house to see if he's here," Tom said quietly.

Jett shook his head. "He's gone. If he wasn't, we'd be dead already."

"I'll call it in. We'll set up roadblocks on all the major roads out of town."

"He'll expect that. He'll take back roads."

"Well, where do you think he'll go?"

"If I knew, we'd be in the car already."

Although he didn't want to, Jett made himself walk toward the master bedroom. He didn't want to see what Blake had done to his ex-wife. He knew it was going to be bad. Georgette had done the one thing he could never tolerate—she'd walked away and taken his child with her.

The scene before him when he entered the bedroom was unlike anything he had ever seen before—and he had been to a lot of murder scenes in his years as an FBI agent.

Georgette lay in the bed. Naked. There were what looked like literally hundreds of small cuts all over her body from her feet to her face. Besides the strong smell of the blood, the room also smelled of bleach.

Only Blake hadn't used it to clean.

He must have used the bleach to pour on the wounds he inflicted on Georgette, causing her untold amounts of pain before he finally slit her neck from ear to ear.

Even in death, Georgette's face was a twisted mask of agony.

There was one more smell that lingered in the death-soaked room.

Urine.

No doubt, Georgette had wet herself either during the torture she suffered before death or after she died. But Jett's gaze was drawn to a small puddle on the floor by the far wall.

"He made her watch."

Anger boiled inside him.

How could Blake do that to his own daughter?

Laila was only nine—what he'd made her watch would have scarred her for life.

Anger equaling his own burned in Tom's eyes. He was a father now, a good one, and he was no doubt picturing what he would do to anyone who hurt Noelle the way Blake had hurt Laila.

Blake hadn't cleaned up the room. It was the first time he hadn't taken forensic countermeasures and made sure he didn't leave any evidence behind. They hadn't linked Blake's murders together until the fourth one. He had targeted different types of criminals, killed them in different ways, made sure he didn't leave anything behind. But when four suspects from cases the two of them had worked turned up dead, they finally realized what Blake was doing.

Since he hadn't bothered with his usual routine, Jett had to believe there was a clue here somewhere. Something that would point to Blake's next move. Blake was a meticulous planner; he had to know where he was going and made arrangements to get himself, Laila, and Violet there. He just had to find out what those arrangements were.

As he scanned the room searching for anything that might point him in the right direction, his eyes fell on the scissors laying on the carpet by the puddle of urine where Laila had wet herself watching her father kill her mother.

Scissors.

Blake wouldn't have hurt Laila, which meant he used them for something else.

Probably to cut duct tape.

And if he was cutting duct tape where Laila had been standing, then it must have been to bind her.

If he was simply fleeing with his child and Violet, then he wouldn't really need to tie Laila up. She was just a little girl and not a threat to him. And she would be scared and upset after what she had witnessed, so he would probably want to keep her close by.

Unless he had something else to do.

"He's going after Savannah before he flees."

* * * * *

3:53 A.M.

"How are you feeling?"

Savannah looked up to see her brother looming over her. Everything that happened tonight still felt a little surreal. If it weren't for the aches and pains and the lingering taste of Jett on her lips, then she would be tempted to believe she dreamed the whole thing. She, Jett, and Sawyer could have died. They were lucky to have walked away with nothing more serious than a few bumps and bruises and cuts. "How are *you* doing?"

"I'm not the one who fell down a flight of stairs," Sawyer said, dropping down onto the couch beside her and picking up her hand. "You need some painkillers?"

"No, I'm fine, Sawyer; stop fussing." She really was feeling fine. She was sore, but she hardly even registered it. She was more worried about Jett. He'd gone over to Blake's ex-wife and daughter's house, and she was worried that it was a trap, and Blake was going to be lying in wait to kill him.

The thought of Jett not coming home alive was tormenting her

She didn't want to keep thinking about it, but she couldn't stop.

She couldn't get the images of his dead body out of her mind.

Just a few days ago, she hadn't even been thinking about Jett, and now, she couldn't imagine him not being a part of her life.

Was this what true love was all about?

That you could never forget about the person, that even if you weren't together, they were still a part of you, that you could pick things back up where they'd left off despite everything that had happened and find a way to work it out.

She never should have let Jett go. She never should have been so upset she hadn't even given him a chance to explain. And she shouldn't have walked out of Jett's house last night because he'd done what he had to do to save his ex's life. Although not on purpose, she had been selfish, and she'd disregarded Jett's feelings when she knew he was a good guy who would never intentionally hurt her. She shouldn't have been so hard on him. It was a mistake she could never undo.

And now Jett might die before they even got a chance to talk properly and resolve things.

"Jett's not going to die."

Savannah looked at her twin. He always knew what she was thinking. But that didn't mean he was right. "You can't know that."

"I can."

"You can't."

"Jett is smart and well trained. And he's not there alone. Tom is with him."

Her brother had intended that to be a comfort, but instead, it added to her anxiety. Tom was a dad now, but Blake wouldn't hesitate to take him out if he perceived him to be a threat. She didn't even want to think about Tom and Hannah's beautiful baby girl growing up without a father. She knew what that was like.

"Are you ever going to believe that Dad's death wasn't your fault?"

She looked into her brother's blue eyes. Their father's eyes. Both she and Sawyer had inherited their father's blue eyes. In the early days after his death, she hadn't been able to look at her brother without seeing her father. Back then, she'd hated it, but now she liked it. It was like a little piece of their dad lived on in his son.

In answer to her brother's question, no. She could never not blame herself for his death. Who else was there to blame?

Short answer. No one.

"Sav, you have to let it go. Dad wouldn't want you beating yourself up about an accident that happened eighteen years ago."

Tears brimmed in her eyes as she remembered their father. He had been the best dad a child could ask for. He worked hard, but he was always there to tuck her and Sawyer into bed each night and read them a bedtime story. On weekends, he would take them to the park, fishing, bike riding, hiking, or the pool. He came to every recital or concert or game they had. He was always there for them.

Yet, when he needed her the most, she hadn't been there for him.

"It was an accident, Savannah."

"No, it wasn't."

"Yes, it was," Sawyer said firmly. "Dad lost control of the car on the wet roads, and it hit a tree."

As though a switch had been flipped, images flowed through her mind.

The sound of the rain on the roof of the car.

Watching the droplets chase each other down the windows.

The car fishtailing across the road.

Her father yanking on the wheel.

The force of the crash vibrating through her body.

Pain bloomed through her.

Then, blackness.

What she saw when she woke up was the most horrible sight she ever had the misfortune to witness.

"Savannah."

Sawyer's hand closed over her shoulder, and he shook her. The movement snapped her out of her reverie. She was breathing way too quickly, and she had curled her hands into fists so tightly she could feel her nails cutting into her skin. The physical pain soothed her a little, and she didn't uncurl her fingers.

She'd been in the back seat when the car crashed, which was probably the only reason she had survived.

A branch had come through the windshield, piercing her father's chest.

There was blood everywhere.

But he wasn't dead.

She could hear him groaning. The sound was almost inhuman. She still heard it in her dreams, and sometimes even while she was awake.

Her seat belt had been jammed, but she'd managed to climb out from it to get to him. When her father had seen she was awake, he had tried to mask his pain, but he couldn't hide it from her. She could see it in his eyes, she could hear it in the way he breathed, she could feel it coming off him.

"You're bleeding." Sawyer uncurled her fingers and blotted at the small bloody crescents with a tissue. "You tried to help him, Savannah. You walked two miles through the pouring rain—injured—to try to get him help."

She'd had a dislocated shoulder, a broken hand, a broken nose, and several cuts and bruises. None of those injuries had stopped her from walking those two miles.

Savannah didn't even remember it.

The rain had drenched her and chilled her to the bone. She'd lost one of her shoes somewhere along the way, and she remembered the pain of broken sticks and rocks cutting into her foot as she walked.

The closest house had been two miles from the site of the accident, and the relief she'd felt when she finally saw a light shining in the dark night had almost caused her knees to give out.

When she'd knocked on the door, and the couple inside had opened it, she'd been so cold and so scared that she'd barely been able to tell them what had happened. They had called 911, then wrapped her up in blankets and bundled her in their car so that she could lead them back to where her father was waiting for her.

Only he wasn't waiting anymore.

She was too late.

He was already dead.

If only she had been a little quicker, found help sooner, walked faster, tried harder, something, anything.

"He didn't die because of you, Savannah. There was nothing you could have done to change what happened that night. You don't have to keep trying to make up for it."

Her head knew her brother was right, but her heart vehemently disagreed.

It was like it believed if she could save enough people, she could somehow make up for not saving her father.

"Whenever I think of him, I see him like he was the last time I saw him," she said quietly. "I wish I could forget that and remember him the way he always was. I don't want to keep seeing him that way."

"I'm sorry, Sav. I wish I could take away those images, but at least you got to say goodbye."

That was true.

She'd been able to say goodbye and that she loved him one more time before she'd gone off to try to find him help. And failed.

"I'm sorry, Sawyer."

"I don't want you to be sorry, Savannah. I never did, and neither did Mom. No one did. No one but you blamed you. It wouldn't have mattered if you'd gotten help quicker; he wouldn't have survived anyway. If you keep trying to save other people because you couldn't save Dad, all you're going to do is wind up dead too."

Sawyer was right. She knew that. She kept putting herself in danger because she wanted—needed—to save someone, only she kept failing. She hadn't saved the woman being kidnapped four years ago, and she hadn't saved Violet Fisher. How many more times was she going to risk her life to save someone before it caught up with her and she ended up dead?

If she was alone, then she might have kept doing it forever, believing her death would be no great loss. But now she and Jett were getting back together, it wasn't fair to him to keep endangering herself.

Savannah was about to admit as much to her brother when gunfire suddenly erupted outside her house.

"Go hide. Now," Sawyer ordered, pulling out his weapon.

There was no way in hell she was doing that. Instead, she

pulled out her own gun.

Sawyer sighed. "What did we just talk about? Stop putting yourself in danger."

"This isn't like that. I know how to shoot, and I can't let you risk your life to keep me safe."

"I'm a *bodyguard*. It's my job."

"But you're more than that to me. You're my brother."

"It's *you* he wants."

"But he'll go after anyone who stands in his way. You try to stop him getting to me, and he will kill you without a second thought." Sawyer could argue with her all he wanted, but she wasn't going to run and hide while people put their lives on the line for her.

Before they could argue further, flames sprung to life outside the windows.

* * * * *

4:08 A.M.

"That's gunshots."

The bottom dropped out of his world.

Gunshots could mean only one thing.

Blake had gone after Savannah, just as he'd thought he would.

"Drive faster," Jett ordered Tom, wishing that he had insisted on driving.

"I'm going as fast as I can to get us there in one piece."

As far as he was concerned, it wasn't fast enough. Jett was perfectly happy to risk life and limb if it meant getting to Savannah even seconds quicker. He would never forgive himself if she was killed because he couldn't stop hunting Blake.

"There are already agents there," Tom reminded him. "And Sawyer is with Savannah. As far as we know, she's safe. Let's not jump to conclusions. The shots could have been our agents; they could already have Blake in custody."

That was true, but his gut said it wasn't.

His gut said that Blake was too smart to get himself shot.

He was starting to get worried that he wasn't going to win this.

Blake could kill the only woman Jett had ever loved and then escape with Violet and Laila, never to be seen again.

He had always been so sure that, sooner or later, Blake would slip up, and he'd catch him, but now he didn't think he would. Blake was just too smart, and he planned ahead. He always knew exactly what he was doing and seemed to have backup plans for his backup plans. When killing Savannah hadn't worked tonight, he hadn't missed a beat. He'd just moved on and killed Georgette and kidnapped his daughter. How could Jett beat someone so calm and prepared?

"Jett."

"What?"

"I see fire."

His brain desperately fought against the inevitable, trying to come up with plausible scenarios for a fire that had nothing to do with Savannah. Only, none of them were really all that plausible.

"I know, I know, drive faster," Tom muttered, flooring the accelerator, and two minutes later, they turned into Savannah's street, and his nightmares became reality.

Dead bodies lay in the street.

Two agents were behind a car, one of them holding his hand to his shoulder, the other aimed a gun on Blake Sedenker.

His ex-partner stood in front of Savannah's house, his daughter in his arms as a human shield, and Violet Fisher stood behind him.

Flames encircled Savannah's house.

A house that would be her grave if he couldn't get her out of there in the next few minutes.

"ETA on the fire trucks is twelve minutes," Tom told him.

Twelve minutes was too long. Savannah and Sawyer would be

dead by then. Last time he'd tried talking Blake into giving himself up hadn't worked, and he wasn't very hopeful this time he would get a different outcome.

A plan began to form in his head.

Maybe all wasn't lost yet.

"Park over there," he instructed Tom, who promptly followed his instructions and parked the car just outside Savannah's house. "He will shoot you, so try to stay out of sight. I don't want to tell Hannah that her husband is dead." Savannah might die because of him; he certainly didn't want to tell a new mother that she'd be raising her baby daughter on her own.

Carefully, he slid out of the car, making sure to keep down and behind the relative safety of the bulletproof vehicle. Blake wouldn't hesitate to fire off a shot first chance he got, just like he wouldn't.

Tom slid out of the car behind him, and Jett hoped that he listened and stayed out of the way. He hoped *everyone* stayed out of his way. The most help the other agents on the scene could be was making sure the residents stayed safely inside their houses and out of harm's way. He wanted his ex-partner's attention focused on him and only him; it was the only way this might work.

"If she's not dead already, Jett, you better pray she is before the fire gets her," Blake shouted out, firing off a shot at the car.

He couldn't let himself get distracted.

Fear for Savannah was threatening to crush him, and it was only by the thinnest of thin threads that he was holding it back.

Ignoring Blake altogether, he said, "Violet, come over here."

Even in the eerie light of the flames, he could see Violet's indecision. She wanted to get as far away from Blake as she could, but she was afraid to cross the man who she had already witnessed, causing death and destruction to so many others, including her own family.

"Don't move a muscle, Violet," Blake ordered.

"He can't grab you, Violet," Jett continued. "If he moves his daughter even a millimeter, one of the agents training a gun on him is going to shoot him. Come over here now."

Violet hesitated, still unsure.

"Even if you run, Violet, I'll track you down. My old partner there, he knows he can't beat me. No one can. So, you can run, but you can never hide. I will find you, and I'll punish you. I don't think you want that, do you now?"

He was losing.

Time was quickly running out.

He had to get Violet to come to him. If he couldn't, he was never going to distract Blake long enough to get him to loosen his hold on his daughter. He only needed one shot.

But if he couldn't get Violet to provoke Blake into letting down his guard, then neither he nor Savannah were going to survive the night.

Violet was scared and traumatized; she had witnessed a lot and had who knows what done to her. Right now, her main concern was staying alive, and she was too afraid to do anything that might bring down Blake's wrath upon her.

There was only one thing he could think of that might spur Violet into actually doing something.

"Violet, Peta is still alive."

Even above the roar of the fire, he could hear her gasp.

"You're lying," Blake snarled, firing off another shot, which bounced off the pavement right beside his knee.

"The bullet pierced her skull, but somehow, it deflected off the bone. She's alive and in the hospital. She was in critical condition at first, but she's doing better. If you come over here, we can take you to her."

"Don't listen to him!" Blake yelled at her, but it was too late, Violet had already taken a few steps in his direction.

The control freak that he was, Blake grabbed for her, unwilling to let his newest toy go.

Jett didn't hesitate.

He took the shot.

The bullet hit his target dead on.

Blake dropped like a rock.

"Get Laila and Violet away from the fire," Jett screamed over his shoulder as he ran toward the house.

The flames were everywhere, claiming everything in their path. He circled the house, looking for a gap in the flames so he could get inside.

Only there wasn't one.

It looked like the outside of the house had been doused in an accelerant of some sort. This time, it didn't seem like Blake had attempted to be subtle. His car sat in the driveway, and it looked like he had just driven up, used his nine-year-old as a human shield, and started shooting as the agents came for him. He must have used Violet to start the fire. The whole thing was very unlike Blake. Maybe torturing Georgette the way he had unlocked something inside him, changing him.

How was he going to get in?

He couldn't see Savannah or Sawyer ... were they already dead?

Was he too late?

The flames underneath a back window appeared to be a little smaller, and Jett scanned the area for something he could use to smash the glass.

Just as he was picking up a potted plant, something slammed into him.

"You think you can take my daughter and the woman I love away from me?" Blake growled as his fist connected with his jaw.

How was Blake still alive?

He'd shot him straight through the heart.

Bulletproof vest.

It was the only thing that made sense.

The force of the bullet slamming into his chest must have momentarily knocked him out.

Blake wasn't winning this time. He may not be dead, but he soon would be. This man was a menace to every single person he came into contact with. Jett couldn't believe he had ever looked up to him, admired him, wanted to learn from him.

Now all he wanted was to be free of him.

As long as Blake was alive, then he and Savannah were never going to be safe, and neither would Violet or Laila.

While Blake continued to pummel him, Jett reached inside his pocket and pulled out his keys. On them was a small Swiss Army Knife. He pulled out the blade and shoved it into Blake's neck, severing his carotid artery.

Blake's eyes grew wide with shock, and then glazed over, and his life dripped out of him with every drop of blood that fell.

Shoving the now limp body of Blake Sedenker to the ground, Jett didn't bother sparing him another glance. Retrieving the potted plant he had dropped when Blake hit him, he threw it through the closest window.

"Jett, you can't go in there," Tom said, appearing at his side. "Fire trucks will be here in three minutes."

"If she's still alive, she won't survive another three minutes in there. Check he's really dead this time." He gestured his head in Blake's direction. The man seemed to have nine lives, and he didn't want him popping back up again.

"It's suicide to go in there," Tom said.

He didn't care.

If Savannah died, then he was as good as dead anyway.

Covering his face with his jacket, he climbed through the smashed window.

Inside, the air was thick with smoke, and he could barely see anything. How could Savannah have survived in here for almost ten minutes?

Fear and despondency threatened to render him useless, but he shoved it aside. He had to find her. Her house wasn't large: a living room, a kitchen diner, three bedrooms, and two bathrooms.

He was in one of the spare bedrooms that was set up as a home office, but he didn't expect to find her in here. She and Sawyer would either have been in the living room talking or in their beds asleep.

Finding his way to the hall, he bypassed the other bedrooms to make his way to the living room. He knew Savannah, and he knew that she wouldn't be able to sleep after what had happened earlier. She would have been too worried about him. She and her brother would likely have been up talking when the fire started, and they found themselves trapped inside the burning house.

The smoke was starting to choke him. It sucked the oxygen out of the room and was smothering him slowly. Much longer in here, and he was going to be dead.

He made it to the living room, but he didn't see Savannah or Sawyer.

Had he been wrong?

Was she in bed?

If he'd made the wrong call, it could have cost her her life.

Jett was sure he was right. Savannah wouldn't have gone to bed. Maybe she and Sawyer had been in the kitchen.

Crossing the hall, he swung the door open and found them.

They were both lying on the floor, no doubt there because they knew to keep low to the ground because the smoke would rise to the ceiling. Their heads were covered, and when he dropped down beside them, he saw that they had used wet towels to cover their mouths and noses to filter out as much smoke as they could.

Jett's hand was shaking as he touched it to Savannah's neck.

"Please be alive, please be alive, please be alive," he muttered the mantra over and over.

Sometimes, life was good to him. Savannah had a pulse. He turned to Sawyer and found Savannah's brother alive as well.

There was no way he could get them both back to the window, especially with the smoke already affecting him.

Quickly, he swung Savannah up into his arms. He'd get her out and then come back for her brother.

Tom was waiting for him outside the window and held out his arms to take Savannah.

Although he didn't want to let her go ever again, he handed her limp body over to Tom, feeling a piece of him stay with her when he relinquished his hold.

"Have to go back for Sawyer," he said, his voice hoarse.

Sirens filled the air.

The fire trucks.

Help was here.

"Let the professionals get him," Tom said.

Leaving the house knowing someone was still inside nearly killed him, but he knew his partner was right. If he went back for Sawyer, they could both die. The firefighters would be able to retrieve him quicker and more safely than he could.

He dragged himself out the window, noticing that the flames in this spot had diminished. Tom must have done something to douse them, although what, he was too tired to figure out. Jett knew he was close to crashing.

When he was out of the house, he reached for Savannah and took her in his arms.

He had to hold her.

He needed to be close to her.

Sinking to his knees, Jett clutched Savannah tightly against his chest, the thumping of her heart reassuring him that she was alive.

Alive.

Her heart still beat.

Her lungs still breathed.

She was alive.

He hadn't lost her.

He would never lose her.

He would never let her go ever again.

* * * * *

7:21 P.M.

Savannah was missing him already.

Jett had dropped her off at Sawyer's house only an hour ago, and she hadn't been able to do anything other than think about him since.

They had been together ever since he had carried her out of her burning home.

She had woken up in his arms and immediately began to choke on the fresh air. If she and Sawyer hadn't covered their faces, they probably wouldn't have still been alive by the time Jett found them.

He had walked through a burning building for her.

If that wasn't true love, then she didn't know what was.

Knowing that Jett would risk his life for her didn't change how she felt about him. She had already known there wasn't anything he wouldn't do for her, and that was why she loved him, although knowing he braved the flames and smoke just for her made her feel all tingly inside.

Tingly in a good way.

A *very* good way.

The kind of way that wished that Jett would hurry up and get back here.

An ambulance had shown up moments after she woke up, and most of the next hour or so were fairly fuzzy in her memory. All she had known was that Jett was beside her holding her hand.

What happened hadn't really sunk in yet.

At the moment, they were just a series of facts in her brain. Facts she had yet to process. She knew at some point she would have to, and that her emotions were going to have to get involved at some point, when they did it wouldn't be pretty. Her house was destroyed, along with everything in it. There were photos of her and her dad in there and special mementos from her childhood that were irreplaceable.

She had lost a lot today, and she wasn't looking forward to experiencing the roller coaster of feelings that would come as soon as the shock wore off.

For now, though, she was just going to relish being alive, and she had Jett to thank for it. He had done more than just carry her out of her smoke-filled, flame-ringed home; he had given her a reason to be happy again. She hadn't had that in a long time. Even before her second assault, she had just been going through the motions. She hadn't been happy since before she and Jett broke up. Although at the time she'd thought ending things with him was the right thing to do, it didn't mean she'd liked it.

But now she had him back, and she could barely contain her joy. Savannah hoped it was enough to bring her through the trauma of today's events.

Sawyer's doorbell rang, and she smiled.

She knew who it was going to be.

"Should I get that?" she asked her brother, wincing as speaking aggravated her throat. It was raw from all the smoke, and each breath raked like hot coals against her tender airways.

"Yep." Sawyer grinned at her, but she could tell from his small wince that his throat was just as sore as hers was. They'd both spent the day in the hospital being monitored and then released an hour ago. Her brother said she could stay with him for as long as she needed to, and as grateful for the offer as she was, she was hoping another offer might be coming soon.

As quickly as she could, she got off the couch and into her wheelchair and rolled herself to the door. When she flung it open, she found exactly who she had expected.

Jett.

Looking too perfect to be true.

Her eyes misted. She didn't deserve this second chance with Jett, but she was so glad she had it.

"Are you crying?" Jett asked, his face creasing with concern.

"Mmhmm." She nodded, brushing at her wet eyes.

"Good tears or bad tears?" He looked uncertain now, unsure what he should do. Jett wasn't good with crying women.

"Good tears," she assured him. "I'm just glad to see you."

"Well, that makes two of us because I'm glad to see you too." He stooped and pressed a quick kiss to her lips while he glanced over her shoulder at her brother. He clearly wanted privacy. She did too. "Dinner?"

"Another date?" she asked hopefully.

"The last one ended rather abruptly."

It had.

Because she'd gotten all bent out of shape over Jett risking his life and his job to save someone he cared about.

"This one won't," she promised.

"I know it won't." The sexy lilt to his voice had her shivering, and it had nothing to do with the cold night.

"See you tomorrow, Sav," Sawyer said knowingly, and a little distractedly. Her brother seemed in an awful hurry to get rid of them, and she wondered whether Ashley was coming over. She really hoped her brother got the same happy ending she had.

"Let's go." Jett swung her into his arms, and she entwined her arms around his neck, holding on to him as he carried her downstairs and outside to his car.

Just like last time, the journey to Jett's house was a silent one. Only, this time, it wasn't an awkward silence; it was a companionable one. They didn't need to talk. They were both content just to enjoy being together again.

"Oh." She looked around in surprise when Jett carried her inside. She had expected to see a recreation of last night's date that hadn't ended as she'd hoped.

Instead, the living room was empty.

"This way." Jett smirked.

He took her into the dining room where he'd set up a candlelit dinner. Rose petals in an array of colors were scattered across the floorboards. Mixed with the scent of the roses was the smell of peaches. If she hadn't known better, she would have thought he'd baked something with peaches for dessert, but Jett knew that it was her favorite candle fragrance.

More tears blurred her vision.

"Are you crying again?"

"This was our first date," she whispered. "You cooked me dinner in your apartment the first night I was released from the hospital. You had the colorful rose petals, and somehow you found out that peach-scented candles were my favorite."

"This is our second first date, and this time we're going to do it right."

"I'm sorry. I owed it to you to give you a chance to explain why you hadn't been there that day after everything you'd done for me."

"I don't want your apologies, Savannah. I just want you." He set her down on one of the chairs. "I couldn't honor your wishes and stay away from you. Last Christmas, when you were in the hospital, I was there. I've been keeping tabs on you since we broke up. I know that sounds kind of stalker-y when I say it out loud, but I couldn't not know what was going on with you. When I heard you'd been hurt, I dropped everything to go to the hospital to check on you. I sat beside your bed while you were unconscious. I held your hand, but when you woke up, I left. And now it's Christmas again, and here we are together again."

She smiled and lifted her hand to tangle her fingers in his soft dark hair. "Christmas miracles."

He leaned his forehead against hers. "I stayed away because I didn't think you wanted me around, but now I don't care what you want. I'm not going anywhere."

"Oh?" She tilted her head so she could kiss him. "You don't care what I want? That's a shame because what I want right now is you, upstairs, in much less clothing."

Jett laughed. "That's my old Savannah. I missed you so much."

She'd missed herself too.

She'd missed this. Just hanging out, having fun, feeling alive, feeling free and light and happy, and not like the hermit, she had slowly been turning herself into.

She didn't want to be that person. She wanted to be her old self. She wanted her hopes and dreams back. She wanted her life back. She wanted to get up each morning excited about the day and not dreading it and counting the hours until she could return to bed. She wanted to be excited for the holidays so she could celebrate with the people she loved. She wanted to get married and have kids. She wanted it all.

"So, you want to go upstairs, huh?" He took her hand and lifted it to his mouth, pressing a kiss to the inside of her wrist, and she practically melted right then and there. For some reason, that did crazy things to her libido.

Instead of picking her up and taking her upstairs to his bedroom, Jett trailed a line of kisses up her arm to her elbow, and she groaned. If he kept this up, he was going to push her over the edge just from a few kisses. It had been so long that it wasn't going to take much to get her there, but she didn't want to come until Jett was inside her. She didn't care that bruises covered half her body; she didn't care that the headache from her concussion still hadn't completely dissipated; she didn't care that her throat hurt with every breath she took and every word she spoke, and she didn't care that her lungs still felt like they were clogged with smoke. She wanted this more than she wanted anything else in the world right now.

"Jett," she implored, pleading with her eyes for him to have mercy on her.

"Beg me." He raised a half teasing, half serious eyebrow.

She was already so desperate that she was ready to do just about anything. She squirmed in her seat and uttered the words she knew would get her what she wanted. "Please, Jett. Take me upstairs now. I want you—no, I *need* you inside me. Now. Right now."

Finally, his mouth was on hers, giving her temporary relief from the clawing need growing inside her. She and Jett, their bodies joined together, their hearts joined together, their lives joined together.

It seemed like she really was about to get her very own Christmas miracle.

* * * * *

8:42 P.M.

"Again?" Jett asked as he held himself propped up on his elbows above Savannah's body.

He couldn't take his eyes off her. She was beautiful, but his gaze kept falling to her bruises. He could have lost her so many times in the last few days alone. He kept trying to let it go, but every breath she took was more of a harsh wheeze that looked like it was causing her pain, and it just kept hammering it in. Blake had almost succeeded in killing her. If he had, then Jett would've had nothing.

Blake was dead, and Savannah was safe—for now, at least. But Jett was an FBI agent. He worked crimes every day of his life. He knew just how many evil people there were in the world and any one of them could wind up taking Savannah from him.

Was he prepared to spend each day with her knowing he could lose her?

Although the prospect of loving her and losing her was a terrifying one, the prospect of living without her was worse.

"What's wrong?" Savannah asked, looking up at him, small lines creasing her forehead.

Sometimes, love was hard.

He had loved his father, and he'd left them. Left his wife and seven kids to fend for themselves without a second thought.

There was no way that wasn't going to influence his outlook on life.

Savannah had a bad habit of putting herself in dangerous situations. Jett knew why she did it, it was because she was trying to make up for being unable to save her father. She was going to do it again. He knew she was. Sooner or later, she would feel compelled to make an attempt to save someone else.

Part of him wanted to lean down, cover her body with his own, cocooning her in a little bubble of safety, and let his weight rest on her, crushing her a little so she could feel just a tiny bit of the weight of the fear that was crushing him. If she wasn't hurt, he might actually do it. Jett wanted her to know just how much she meant to him and how destroyed he would be if anything happened to her.

He was the strong one, the responsible one, the tough one, and Jett believed he was all of those things. But there was also the scared, abandoned thirteen-year-old boy inside him too. And that boy didn't want anyone else he loved to just drop out of his life.

"Jett, you're scaring me." Savannah wiggled backward and propped herself up on her elbows

"Sorry." He forced a smile to his lips. Worrying her was the last thing he wanted to be doing right now. This was supposed to be a happy day; they were back together, and they had just made love. Blake was dead now and no longer a threat and he could take a couple of days off so they could celebrate Christmas together. Maybe he should just let this go for now—they didn't have to sort everything out overnight. They had time; they had the rest of their lives.

Lowering his mouth to hers, he tried to kiss her again, but she pushed him away. "Don't try to distract me. Is something wrong? Did you change your mind? Do you not want us to get back together? Was this just about—?"

"Savannah, stop." He held his finger to her lips to silence her. Although it was hard for him to show any vulnerability this time, it was probably unavoidable if he and Savannah were going to have a future. "No more putting yourself in dangerous situations, okay, sweetheart?" he asked, bearing his insecurities for the first time in their relationship.

"Is that what you're worried about?"

"More than worried. I can't lose you, Savannah."

"Sawyer and I were talking about that before the fire." She shuddered as she said the word, and he moved to sit beside her, wrapping an arm around her shoulders and tugging her to rest against his chest. "I'll try to accept that my father's death wasn't my fault. I'll try to curb my subconscious need to save others because I couldn't save him." She twisted, so her blue eyes pinned his green ones. "I promise you that I won't ever recklessly put myself in danger."

Jett felt himself relax.

That was exactly what he had needed to hear.

His hand brushed up and down her arm, his fingertips whispering across her breast, and he felt her shiver against him. A good shiver this time.

Before he could take things further, she sat up and straddled him, but her expression wasn't filled with lust; it was earnest.

"You have to promise me the same thing, Jett. I lost my dad; I don't want to lose you too. I know you have a dangerous job, and I'm not asking you to quit it or anything, but you have to promise me that you will *always* be careful."

That promise was easy to make.

His hands grasped her hips, and he held her still as he leaned up to kiss her. He didn't think she realized what she'd just done. She had moved herself to straddle him without a second thought of her injured hip. From the tightness in her jaw and the way she held her weight mostly on her good side, he knew she was in pain, but she seemed to still have reasonable movement in the joint. He was sure she could still walk—she was just scared to see if it could bear her weight.

Tonight was about the two of them reconnecting, but tomorrow he was going to push her to get out of that wheelchair and try walking again.

Because of the awkward way she was perched on his stomach, he lifted her and flipped her over, so she was lying on her back again. Now he had full access to every single part of her, and he intended to make sure he left no inch of her untouched.

Jett took her nipple into his mouth, and she moaned and lifted her chest to give him better access. Last time they'd made love it had been hot and fast and a fiery mess of emotions that had built up over the two and a half years since they'd broken up. This time, he wanted to go slow and savor every single second.

* * * * *

10:50 P.M.

Sometimes, people really made things easy for him.

Was that a good thing?

For him, it was. For them, not so much.

He waited a good five minutes after the woman disappeared inside the building before making his move.

He wasn't worried about being seen. It was late, almost eleven, and there were only four people he'd seen in the parking lot. One was a homeless man asleep in a sleeping bag over in the far corner. If the man even survived the cold night, he wouldn't be telling anyone what he saw, if the numerous beer bottles scattered around him was any indication. There was also a man with a prostitute parked in an SUV under a streetlight. If he were them, he would have picked a darker corner. Neither of them was likely to talk, should anyone even figure out they were here tonight. The last person in the parking lot was a man in a black hoodie who was hanging around the door with his hands shoved in his pockets, waiting to rob the patrons as they exited the bookie.

Again, this man wasn't going to be talking to the cops.

It may even work out in his favor that the thief was here. He would provide a potentially viable suspect when the police finally did arrive on the scene.

No one would be looking for him.

Just the way he liked it.

Just the way it should be.

He always took care to make sure there was no one about who would witness anything that might lead the cops to him.

Being careful was a way of life when you did what he did. You were either careful, or you got caught. And when you got caught, you were thrown in prison.

Lucky for him, he knew how to play the game.

Be remorseful, follow the rules, pretend to recognize that what you did was wrong and promise to change. Shrinks were easier to fool than you might at first think. They wanted to believe that a piece of good, no matter how small, lived inside every person and that if you could just get ahold of it you could make it grow and change the person from evil to good.

Too bad for them, some people didn't have any good inside them. All that lived inside him was needs—needs that he would satisfy no matter what. And if he had to play a certain game to regain his freedom, then he would do it. He *had* done it, and now he was free and able to satisfy those needs.

It had been a long time.

So long that he was almost ready to explode.

If he wasn't such a careful person, then he would have just jumped straight back into old habits. But he was always careful. Always. It was the only way to ensure he survived.

He had only ever made one mistake.

One mistake that had led to his incarceration.

But now he was free, and he could return to the life he'd had before. He had waited a year. A *whole* year. It was the only way to make sure no one suspected him ever again.

Now he could get what he wanted and take care of some old business, and then he could finally put the past behind him.

This time, he was going to do things differently. He was going to make sure that he never made another mistake that led to his capture. He had acknowledged the mistakes he made, and he had thought up ways to rectify them and modify his plans, so it never happened again.

If you couldn't learn from your mistakes, then you were doomed to repeat them.

With a last glance around, he climbed out of his car and circled around the lot to the other side of the bar so he could enter through the front door. Without pausing, he strode through and then came out the back door. He headed straight for the car abandoned almost ten minutes ago by the woman who was going to remember today as the day she had made the biggest, most irresponsible mistake of her life.

At the car, he knocked on the window.

The little girl inside startled and looked up from the iPad in her hands.

He hadn't expected the child to just swing the door open when he approached. He was sure that she had been taught never to talk to strangers. Especially when your mother brought you to a bar in the middle of the night and left you in the car while she went in to place bets.

She looked at him suspiciously and shrank away from the window where he was standing. That was fine, he already knew how he was going to get her to open the door.

"Your mom had an accident. She slipped inside and hurt her back. She asked someone to come out and get you." He held back from saying that the mother had said she was worried about her daughter as it didn't seem like something a woman who would abandon her child in a dark parking lot on a cold winter's night would say.

The girl inched closer, her suspicions faltering. "My mom fell?"

He nodded. "Yes. We've called an ambulance, and she said she didn't want you out here when they arrived."

This seemed to convince the child, and he assumed it was because she could picture her mother worrying about how it would look to the paramedics if she was alone out here. The kid was obviously smart if she had figured out that her mother's treatment of her was neglect. He'd have to be careful with this one; he didn't want another too intelligent child ruining things.

"Is she okay?" the girl asked.

"She's in a lot of pain." Going with a hunch, he added, "I think she needs you in there with her."

That seemed to do the trick. He assumed the girl was used to taking care of her mother since it was clear her mother wasn't particularly interested in taking care of her.

Still, a little tentatively, the child unlocked the car and climbed out, reaching behind her to grab her coat and shrug into it. The coat was old and had several patches, and he felt a sudden stab of empathy for the girl. He knew what it was like to grow up with parents who didn't care about you. To go to bed hungry because the money his mother would have spent on food, she spent on drugs instead. To wear old, stained, patched clothes to school where all the other kids would make fun of him.

He would have taken being hungry and dirty any day over what else had happened to him as a child.

But now wasn't the time for reminiscing.

Now wasn't the time for reliving old hurts.

This was the time for him. For what he wanted. To give him some happiness for a change.

He waited until the girl had her coat on and turned to start walking toward the bar before he grabbed her. He whipped an arm out and wrapped it around her waist, yanking her hard up against his body, then pressed his other hand over her mouth and nose. It served a double purpose. It stopped her from screaming for help, and it cut off her airways and would eventually make her pass out.

The girl thrashed in his arms, frantically fighting for her life.

She wouldn't win.

When you were a child, you never won.

It was the prerogative of the older, bigger, stronger adult to win.

He picked up his pace as he spun on his heel and headed for his car. The girl was still fighting—very valiantly for such a small thing—when he reached it, and he had to waste precious seconds waiting for her to pass out before he was able to stuff her in the trunk.

Eventually, she went limp in his arms, and he laid her out gently in the trunk. She was a pretty child; she had a mass of freckles over milky white skin, a wild tangle of red curls framing her face, and although her eyes were closed, he had seen earlier that they were blue.

Blue eyes.

He hated blue eyes.

Hated them.

Already, he could feel his blood beginning to boil.

Unwanted memories began to churn inside him.

They brought anger along with them.

He relished his anger.

In prison, he'd had to clamp down on it, pretend he was reformed, but now he could let it run free again.

It was invigorating.

Freeing.

He finally felt like his old self again.

When he got the kid someplace quiet and secluded, he was going to have to do something about the blue eyes. He was going to be keeping this one for a while, and he didn't want them interfering with things.

Marcus King smiled as he slammed the trunk closed.

It was good to be back.

DECEMBER 24TH

10:23 A.M.

Savannah didn't really want to hand the little bundle in her arms back over.

She had been cuddling Tom and Hannah's five-month-old daughter ever since they'd arrived at Chloe's house over an hour ago. She wanted this; she wanted a baby with Jett. Savannah had always known that she wanted to have a family one day, and it seemed one day had finally arrived.

Chloe and Hannah were talking baby stuff since Chloe was only a couple of weeks away from giving birth, but she wasn't really listening. She was just sitting in Chloe and Fin's living room, holding the baby in her arms, and staring at her in awe. How amazing would it be to hold something that was half her and half the man she loved?

When she'd been giving Noelle a bottle, the baby had stared up at her with big brown eyes, her little hands curling around Savannah's finger, and she had very nearly grabbed Jett, insist they leave immediately and return to bed to get busy creating their own little baby

Logically, she knew it wasn't the right time for them. They needed to work on their relationship first and get them on the right track, and then they could think about bringing a new person into the world. But maybe soon. She and Jett had both admitted their biggest fear to each other last night. They were both afraid they would lose each other, but they couldn't let those fears make them miss out on having something wonderful together.

Something wonderful like a baby.

She smiled down at the infant, who was fast asleep on Savannah's lap, her lashes fanned out on her rosy, plump cheeks, her lips pursed in a sweet little pout. Noelle was a little angel, and Savannah couldn't wait to have a little angel of her own.

"You look good like that," Jett whispered in her ear.

"Yeah?" She smiled up at him.

"Makes me regret we have lunch plans." He winked then brushed a kiss across her lips before straightening.

"I wish we could stay, but we're making Christmas lunch at our house tomorrow, and Hannah wants to get started on some of the cooking today. Plus, we still have to bake cookies for her to put out for Santa Claus tonight," Tom said.

Baking.

It was Christmas Eve. This was usually the day when she would have baked her big gingerbread creation. She had been in the hospital last Christmas and had never made her gingerbread fairground, but she'd already done all her shopping and planning, so she'd had everything she would have needed to make it. For some reason, she hadn't been able to throw them away, even though she didn't have any intention of ever making it, so they'd still been in her house. Now her house was destroyed, and she couldn't have made it even if she wanted to.

Jett was watching her with a funny look on his face like he knew exactly what she was thinking about.

Sometimes it scared her a little that he knew her so well.

"Here you go." She held the baby out to Hannah, who scooped her up and cradled her daughter against her chest, kissing her soft little head.

Yeah, she definitely wanted a baby.

No sleep, midnight feeds, teething, tantrums—she wanted it all.

Holding such a perfect little person in your arms, knowing that they were yours to love, to guide, to watch grow—that would make everything worth it.

Jett's hand grasped hers and squeezed. When she looked up at him, she knew he was in the same place she was. Maybe they didn't need to wait too long to make sure their relationship was on the right track. They knew they loved each other; they knew they had to be open with each other; they knew they wanted a future together. They had their second chance, and neither of them was going to throw it away.

"Merry Christmas, everyone." Hannah grinned. They all knew how Christmas crazy she was.

They all exchanged Christmas hugs and kisses, and Jett and Fin had gone back to the kitchen when she noticed the fluffy, pink bunny laying on the carpet half under the couch.

"Hannah and Tom forgot Noelle's favorite stuffed animal," she said, rolling over to retrieve it.

"I don't think they've left yet," Chloe said, looking out the window.

"We should get it to them before they go. What if Noelle can't sleep without it?" She knew that was unlikely; the baby had already been asleep when she'd left, but she would hate for her to wake and want it later. When she was a little girl, she'd had a wooly lamb that she had taken everywhere with her until she was eight when the kids at school had started to tease her about it. After her father's death, she had started sleeping with it again, only stopping when she went to college.

She still had it.

No.

She didn't.

It had been destroyed along with everything else that had been in her house.

"Savannah? Everything okay?"

"Fine," she said, not wanting to discuss this today. Today was about happiness and the future, not about the past. "We should get this to Hannah and Tom before they finally get all the baby stuff in the car and leave."

"You and Jett want one." Chloe grinned as they headed outside.

"One of what?"

"A baby."

"Maybe," she admitted.

Chloe laughed. "No maybe—you and Jett are back together, and you both want a kid. That's so great. If you get pregnant soon, then our kids will be basically the same age, and they'll be able to grow up together."

Her friend's excitement was contagious, and she decided she and Jett were definitely going to discuss the issue of babies as soon as they got home today. What better time to conceive a baby than Christmas?

Just as they got out the front door, Tom and Hannah's SUV reversed out of the driveway.

"Maybe I can catch them." Chloe jogged across her front lawn to the street and waved frantically, while Savannah rolled across the front porch to use the driveway since the concrete was easier to navigate than the soft grass.

They still didn't have any snow, and tomorrow was Christmas. You couldn't have Christmas without snow, and yet the clear blue sky and watery sunshine hinted that that was exactly what they were going to get this year.

Even without snow, this was still going to be one of the best Christmases she'd ever—

A loud bang pierced the quiet morning.

Just like the ones that had erupted outside her house just before Blake Sedenker set fire to it.

For a moment, she feared he was back.

That somehow, he had managed to survive.

That Jett hadn't killed him.

That he was back to get his revenge.

All of that flew through her mind in a microsecond as her eyes automatically tracked in the direction the shot had been fired from.

A man was standing at the end of the driveway.

He held a gun in his hand.

Chloe lay on the ground.

She wasn't moving.

Before her brain processed what her hands were doing, she was wheeling her chair as quickly as she could toward the man who had just shot her best friend.

"Hey!" she yelled. Jett and Fin were inside; they would have heard the shot, and they'd be here any moment; she just had to delay this man for a few seconds to give them a chance to catch him.

The man turned toward her and did the opposite of what she had expected. She had expected him to fire at her and was prepared to fling herself sideways into the hedge.

Instead, he lowered the gun.

His head cocked to the side as though he was not only surprised to see her but was considering something.

A moment later, she knew what.

Instead of retreating as a normal human being would do, he darted forward. She was only a yard or two away from him by now, and he reached her in just a single step. He yanked her out of her chair and threw her over his shoulder.

The world spun as he swung her around.

How could this be happening?

Just a few minutes ago, she was contemplating having babies and a family with the man she loved. She'd been happy and excited about her future, and for the first time in eighteen years, she was actually beginning to accept her father's death for the accident it was.

Now, her friend lay dead or dying in the street, and she was being kidnapped.

"Savannah!" Jett screamed her name.

For a second, she thought she was saved.

But then more gunshots filled the air.

He was shooting at Jett and Fin.

Marcus King was going to kill Jett and then kidnap her.

* * * * *

11:11 A.M.

His wife lay unmoving on the ground.

His *pregnant* wife lay unmoving on the ground.

His wife had been shot.

His *pregnant* wife had been shot.

The only thing in the world Fin wanted to do right now was go running straight to her to see if she was okay. To perform whatever first aid it took to make sure she didn't die.

Nineteen months ago, he had received a call to tell him his pregnant girlfriend had been in a car accident. That time their baby boy, Christopher, hadn't survived. It had been too early in the pregnancy for his lungs to have developed enough for him to live.

This time, the baby could survive. Chloe was thirty-seven weeks along, which meant the baby would be classified as full-term, so if she went into labor, then the baby should live.

If they both survived the gunshot wound.

"Savannah."

He and Jett had been in the kitchen when they'd heard the gunshots. They had dropped what they were doing, retrieved Chloe's weapons and given one to Jett, then they'd come running outside to find Chloe shot and Marcus King holding Savannah over his shoulder.

His instincts were to go running straight to the woman he loved, and Jett's were no different. But the second Marcus heard them, he turned the gun on them.

Despite the bullets firing in their direction, Jett didn't slow.

He wasn't thinking, he was acting purely on protective instincts, and he was going to go running straight to Savannah.

Launching himself at Jett, he tackled him to the ground, and they rolled behind Chloe's car which was parked on the lawn in front of the house because he'd washed it yesterday afternoon, thanks to Chloe's weird obsession with driving a clean car.

"Let me up." Jett struggled beneath him.

"Stop," he hissed.

"He has Savannah." Jett tried to throw him off.

"He shot Chloe, but you're just going to get yourself killed."

"I can get him," Jett insisted.

Fin debated. If Jett could keep his head on straight, then maybe he really could get off a shot at Marcus King.

The second he levered his body off the FBI agent's, Jett launched to his knees and darted up, firing off a shot.

Bullets continued to fly.

For every one Jett fired, Marcus fired one straight back at them.

They were trapped.

And he was every bit as anxious to get to Chloe as Jett was to get to Savannah.

Tires screeched, the bullets stopped, a door slammed, and then a car engine revved and took off down the street.

The only thing his brain focused on was that Marcus had stopped shooting at them.

Chloe.

He had to get to her.

Stumbling to his feet, he ran.

He heard Jett screaming and firing a weapon. He heard more voices yelling. It all blurred into one.

Chloe lay in a large puddle of blood.

For a moment, that was all he saw.

Blood.

Too much blood.

He tried to breathe deeply, clear away his panic. Pretend Chloe was just another patient who needed him.

His eyes scanned her body in search of the bullet hole that was the cause of all the blood. There was a jagged hole just under her left collar bone. He didn't see anything else.

Yanking his sweater over his head, he balled it up and dropped to his knees beside his wife, pressing it firmly against her wound.

Fin had hoped that the pain of having something held against her wound would be enough to rouse Chloe, but it wasn't.

She just lay there.

Her eyes were closed, but she was still breathing.

Breathing.

He tried to focus on that.

"Come on, Chloe, don't die. Don't do this to me again." Throughout the entire pregnancy, he had been terrified that something would go wrong again. That this was all too good to be true. That not being able to save his son, he was going to be punished and lose this baby too. Now it was all coming true. Chloe had been shot when he was just yards away from her inside the house. He could lose her and their baby all in one horrible fell swoop.

"Ambulance is on the way. What happened?" Tom asked.

"Marcus King," he said tightly. They'd thought the man was no longer a threat since he'd been out of prison for a year and made no attempts to follow through on the threat he'd made against Chloe when she testified against him as a child.

Apparently, they'd been wrong.

"How did he get Savannah?" Jett roared, storming frantically up and down the street.

"Marcus has Savannah?" Tom asked. Fin had no idea why he was back here, but he didn't really care; his focus was on Chloe and the pulse he could feel beating against the side of his hand as he kept pressure on her wound.

"Yes."

"What happened?" Tom asked again.

"Fin and I were in the kitchen when we heard gunshots. We didn't even know Savannah and Chloe were out here; we thought they were still in the living room."

"I made Hannah get out of the car and take Noelle and go inside the gas station when we heard the shots. We were only a couple of blocks away. Marcus jumped into a car when he saw me coming. He must have been here to get his revenge on Chloe, so why take Savannah? What did you see when you came outside?" Tom asked.

"Chloe was on the ground, Savannah's wheelchair was empty, and he had her over his shoulder," Jett sounded wired.

"Noelle's bunny."

"What?" Jett asked.

"We must have left Noelle's bunny behind, and they were bringing it out to us," Tom explained, pointing at something in the driveway behind him.

"He must have been lying in wait for Chloe. He probably waited for you and Hannah to drive off, and then he shot her. If they were trying to catch you before you left, then Chloe probably ran to flag you down. He could have shot her and run, but he didn't. Savannah must have tried to intervene. She couldn't help herself. She probably thought she could buy Fin and me enough time to get out here if she distracted Marcus." Jett sounded a mixture of proud, angry, and terrified.

"She probably saved Chloe's life," he said quietly. The wound to Chloe's shoulder was potentially fatal, but not necessarily so. So long as they got her to the hospital and were able to repair the damage, then both she and the baby would likely survive. If Marcus King had gone to all this trouble to get his revenge, he would have checked to make sure that she was dead before he left.

But Savannah had distracted him.

"And now he has her," Jett said, going quiet.

It made no sense.

Marcus King was a child rapist and murderer; what was he going to do with Savannah?

"Mmm," Chloe groaned as her eyes struggled open.

Fin's attention immediately snapped back to his wife. "Chloe? Can you hear me?"

"Fin?" she mumbled

"Right here, sweetheart, I'm right here." A weight lifted off his shoulders as he touched his lips to her forehead.

"The baby?" Panic filled her brown eyes.

"Is okay," he assured her.

"Marcus."

"Shh," he soothed. Keeping one hand on her wound, with his other, he tenderly brushed a stray lock of hair behind her ear. "Just rest, an ambulance is coming."

"He shot me," she said, sounding surprised.

"He did, but you're going to be okay," he promised. She was awake and talking, the bleeding was slowing—they were both going to be okay.

"Savannah?"

He didn't want to tell her about her friend right now, he didn't want to cause her any anxiety before she was rushed to the hospital and into surgery. But he knew his wife wouldn't want to be kept in the dark. "Marcus took her."

"Took her?" Chloe made a weak attempt at sitting up but barely made it a few inches off the asphalt before she sank back down, wincing in pain. "That hurts."

"I know it does, honey." He pressed harder against the wound, and Chloe flinched again.

"Why would he take her?" Her eyelids were beginning to droop as the effects of blood loss sapped her energy.

"Just rest now, sweetheart," he soothed as he began to stroke her hair. Sirens filled the air, and he relaxed further. He wasn't going to completely relax until he knew for sure that his wife and baby were both okay, but at least he still had them. This could so easily have had a different ending. Last Christmas, he'd gotten a miracle when he got Chloe back, and now he had another.

As he moved to the side to allow the paramedics access to Chloe, he reached for her hand and squeezed it tightly, pleased when she returned the gesture with a weak squeeze of her own.

Fin's gaze fell on Jett.

He was standing staring down the street.

By some miracle, he may still have Chloe and the baby, but Jett had just lost the woman he loved, and he might never get her back.

* * * * *

12:34 P.M.

She was scared and sore, but what was upsetting Savannah the most was that she had already broken the promise she made to Jett.

Just hours ago, they had been lying in bed together after making love, and he'd admitted to her that he was afraid she was going to put herself in danger again and wind up dead. Jett had opened up to her, allowed her to see his more vulnerable side, and she knew what a big deal that was to him. She had promised that she wouldn't do it again. She had promised that she wouldn't make him lose her.

And now, she had.

She had tried to stop Marcus King from running before Jett and Fin got there, and she had failed.

She had tried to save Chloe, and she had failed.

They might all be dead.

Marcus had been firing off shots before he threw her in his car and drove off. For all she knew, Jett, Chloe, the baby, and Fin were all dead.

If Jett had died angry and hurt that she had broken her promise just hours after making it and gotten herself kidnapped, then she didn't think she could survive.

Destroying the only man she had ever loved—would ever love—would destroy her.

Savannah choked on a sob.

How could this be happening?

She was lying on some dirty, disgusting floor, her wrists were tied together behind her back, she was blindfolded, gagged, and he'd stuffed earplugs into her ears. She couldn't see, she couldn't hear, she couldn't scream for help, she couldn't move—she couldn't do *anything,* and it was killing her.

She hated feeling helpless.

It reminded her of the night of the car accident.

Walking along through the pouring rain, wondering if her father was still alive, desperate to find someone, but no one was there.

It didn't matter how far she walked or which direction she had gone in, there was no one.

Only her.

Alone, wet, tired, dirty, and desperate.

Savannah hadn't even realized that she was hurt until the following morning when she awoke in the hospital with her mother lying on the bed with her and holding her in her arms.

Sawyer had been there too.

She hadn't been comforted by their presence because it had been too late.

Her father was already dead, and there was nothing anyone could do to bring him back.

That was how she felt now.

She was alone, Jett could be dead, and there was no one to help her. No one could wave a magic wand and change what was happening, and she didn't know what to expect next.

None of this made any sense.

Marcus King kidnapped and raped little girls between the ages of eight and twelve. What did he want with her? She was definitely not a little girl, and she didn't even meet the physical characteristics of the girls he targeted. Of all of Marcus King's known victims, there wasn't a single blonde among them. Nor did any have blue eyes. He appeared to prefer either brunettes or redheads with brown eyes. So, what was she doing here?

She screamed.

Well, as best as she could with a foul-tasting rag shoved in her mouth.

Even though she knew it was pointless, she couldn't just do nothing. She couldn't just lie here and wait for Marcus to kill her or do whatever horrible thing he had planned.

When she slumped back against the floor, she felt something.

A vibration.

Savannah froze.

Someone was in here with her.

Was it Marcus?

Was he sitting here watching her fall apart, relishing every second of her suffering?

Without her sense of sight and hearing, she only had one left that could help her. Her sense of smell. She drew in a breath through her nose and began to categorize the scents. There were the horrible ones associated with whatever dark, dank place Marcus was hiding out in. She filtered those out and focused on whatever was left.

Lemon shampoo.

Fabric softener.

And bubblegum.

Bubblegum?

Kids loved bubblegum. She and Sawyer had been obsessed with it all through elementary and middle schools. They'd had their favorite flavors and had competitions to see who could blow the biggest bubbles.

Marcus must have taken another child.

That both terrified and strengthened her.

If she could just get the girl to help her out of her bonds, then maybe they actually stood a chance at getting out of here. She knew it was a long shot, and she knew that she was asking a lot of a child who wouldn't be more than twelve, but she had no other choices.

"Please, help me," she said through her gag, hoping it came out clear enough for the child to understand.

The girl must have moved closer because she felt something brush against her leg, and then trace up her body and behind her where her hands were restrained.

"Take out the gag," Savannah said.

There was no more movement, and she started to lose hope. She was balancing precariously on the edge of completely losing it, becoming nothing but a useless, blubbering mess, falling into a shock-induced haze where she would barely be able to function.

The only thing keeping her sane was Jett.

If he was alive, then she had to do everything within her power to get back to him so she could apologize.

All of a sudden, the earplugs were pulled out.

"Can you hear me?" asked a girl.

Since the gag was still in, Savannah nodded.

"You're tied up. Did he take you, or are you another trick?"

She wasn't sure how to answer that since she couldn't really talk, so she settled for shaking her head. This would be so much easier if the girl would just remove the blindfold and gag.

The girl didn't say anything else, and Savannah was afraid that she hadn't believed her. Marcus King must have tricked her somehow when he abducted her. That fit perfectly with his previous MO. He had tried to trick Chloe into getting into his van; if she had, she wouldn't be here today, and Marcus would have remained free, probably killing dozens more children between then and now. Sixteen years in prison wasn't long enough. Marcus should have spent the rest of his life behind bars for what he had done.

Small hands ran up her arms to her face. They fumbled there for a moment before her blindfold fell away. In front of her was a redheaded girl who looked to be about ten. She looked a little malnourished, and the coat she was wearing had several patches on it. Whoever was raising this child didn't look to be doing a very good job.

There was also a strip of material covering her eyes like the one the girl held in her hands.

The girl's thin fingers traced their way down her face to her mouth, then pulled out the gag, and Savannah drew in a deep breath, clearing her lungs of the stale air the gag seemed to have trapped there.

"I'm Savannah. What's your name?" she asked the child.

The girl withdrew her hands and pulled her legs to her chest, wrapping her arms around them and making herself as small as possible. "Payton," she replied in a small voice.

"How old are you, Payton?"

"Ten."

Despite the fact Payton was clearly terrified, there were no tears in her voice. She was holding it together, and that boded well for both of them. "Has he hurt you?" Savannah asked gently.

"No," Payton sniffed. "He just held his hand over my mouth and nose until I couldn't breathe, and then when I woke up, I was in here."

"Here" was a poorly lit room with no windows. There was a bed, table and chairs, a TV on a stand, and a collection of Disney movies that seemed to include every single one ever made, a bookcase crammed full of books, and an overflowing toy box. It looked like Marcus had intended to keep Payton here for a long time. With his previous victims, he had kept them only a few hours before killing them and disposing of their bodies—maybe he wanted to do things differently this time.

"Why are you wearing the blindfold, Payton?" she asked. She needed to scrounge up every bit of information she could if they were going to get out of here. Payton was blindfolded, and yet, she wasn't restrained in any way. She could remove it if she wanted to, but she hadn't. There had to be a reason for that.

"He told me to."

"Why, honey?"

"He said he didn't like blue eyes. That if he saw mine again, he would have to get rid of them."

Well, that wasn't good.

She had blue eyes too.

Maybe there was a reason why he never took a child who had them. They meant something to him. Something bad. If he came in here and found out that she was no longer wearing a blindfold, what would he do to her?

Savannah didn't want to find out.

Payton inched closer. "Are we going to die?"

How did you answer that?

How did you tell a ten-year-old girl that yes, they were both likely going to be tortured and murdered?

She was about to open her mouth to reassure the girl that there was still hope when she heard footsteps.

Marcus was coming.

She better think up a plan quick.

* * * * *

1:16 P.M.

He was losing his mind.

Not knowing what was going on and if Savannah was all right was the worst.

Jett shoved his hands into his pockets and stared out the window. It was a beautiful day. *Too* beautiful. Savannah was gone.

Taken. There shouldn't be blue skies and sunshine; there should be dark gray clouds and howling winds that echoed the aching sense of loss and helplessness that filled him up inside.

Savannah had broken her promise.

She had said no more putting herself in danger, and yet once again, she had.

Was he angry?

Yes.

Was he terrified of losing her?

Yes.

Was he also proud as heck that she had tried to save her friend's life and stop a dangerous child rapist and murderer?

Yes.

Was it all worth it if Savannah died?

That question was harder to answer.

He wouldn't wish Chloe and her baby dead for anything. Nor did he want to see Marcus King abduct and kill more children. But Savannah was *his*; how could he live without her?

That seemed like a stupid thing to feel given that he'd only come back into Savannah's life three days ago, but just because they hadn't been together in nearly three years didn't mean that he had stopped loving her. He should never have waited this long to get her back, he shouldn't have given her time and space, but he had always believed that they would end up together.

And now, they might not.

Should he be grateful that they had one last beautiful night together? Or would it have been better if he'd lost her before they reconnected?

He might never get her back alive.

There was a chance he might not ever even get her body back.

But even if he didn't, he could never be sorry for last night. He would cling to those memories if they were all he'd have left. He'd replay it in his head, keeping a part of her alive.

Jett wished he had told her he loved her.

He had shown her with his body, and he hoped he'd shown her with his actions, but he hadn't said the words. What if he never got a chance to tell her?

This was his worst nightmare come true.

This was what had held him back from fighting for Savannah.

Fear did crazy things to you sometimes. It made you see the world differently; it messed with your head and your heart—made you do things that were completely out of character. Fear took your happiness and made you throw it away because breaking out of its bonds was too hard.

Well, he was going to do it.

He was letting go of the fear.

Yes, he could lose Savannah, either now or sometime in the future, but not having her at all was worse than having her and losing her.

"Chloe should be out of surgery soon." The door to the conference room swung open, and Tom strode inside.

"She's going to make it?"

"She's stable, but she started having contractions, so they had to do an emergency C-section."

"The baby?" Chloe and Fin had already lost one child; he didn't think either of them could cope with losing another. He wouldn't wish that kind of pain on anyone.

Tom smiled. "A boy."

"He's okay?"

"He's doing great. Strong, healthy, perfect. His name is Asher."

Asher; the name meant happy or blessed, and that tiny little baby had certainly blessed his parents and filled them with a happiness he could never understand. Chloe and Fin had lost their first son, Christopher, and while Asher could never replace him or fill the void his death had caused, he could bring them untold amounts of joy and love.

Savannah wanted babies—he'd seen it written all over her face at Chloe and Fin's house this morning when she was holding baby

Noelle in her arms. She'd looked so good with the baby. So happy and relaxed and content. He wanted to give her that. He wanted it for both of them. He wanted to have his baby growing in her stomach; he wanted to hold something that was part of both of them.

To have that first, he needed to get Savannah back alive and in one piece.

"Any news on Marcus yet?" he asked Tom.

"No. Nothing at all since he was released. He visited his parole officer once, and then he just disappeared."

"Aside from the attempted abduction of Chloe when she was ten, the FBI was able to charge him with the rape and murder of four other girls between the ages of eight and twelve."

"There were another seven that the FBI linked him to as well, but there wasn't enough evidence to be able to charge him."

"If Chloe hadn't realized something was wrong and screamed for help rather than walking up to his car, then he probably wouldn't have been found. Once they got the partial license plate, they were able to get his name, and then when they went to his house to interview him, they found photos of some of the dead girls hanging on his walls. From there, they found the girls' blood and hair in his van, and they were able to arrest and later convict him. Before Chloe, he wasn't even on their radar."

"He's good at fitting in," Tom added.

"He is," Jett agreed. "He ran a company that organized and ran children's birthday parties, yet he never abducted any child who attended one."

"He's smart," Tom said as he took a seat at the table.

"Assuming that since he tried to trick Chloe into getting close enough for him to grab her and drive off with her, he did it with all his victims. He must have appeared safe enough for them to willingly walk over to him." Jett joined Tom at the table where every piece of evidence he could retrieve from Marcus's case was spread out.

"Even as a kid, Chloe had a cop's instincts."

"Lucky for her. Most of his victims went missing in the afternoon. He kept them only a few hours before killing them— just long enough for him to sexually assault them before he strangled them, then when it was dark, he left their bodies at the side of freeways. Taking Savannah makes no sense. She's not a kid. What does he want with her?" Not having an answer to that was killing him. If he could get a read on what Marcus was doing, then maybe he could figure out where he was.

"It doesn't fit his MO at all. Being caught, spending sixteen years in prison, it's obviously led to him changing things and going about them a different way. We just need to figure out how Savannah fits into that."

"I've been going through missing children cases, looking for anything that might fit. Sixteen years is a long time. He's a sexual predator; he can't stay away from little girls forever. So far, I haven't found anything that looks like him."

"I might have one," Tom said.

"Who, and when was she taken?"

"Her name is Payton Zubriski. She's ten, and she went missing last night."

"He took her at night?"

"Another change in his MO. Payton was left alone in her mother's car while her mother went into a bar to place some bets."

"Left her alone? What time was it? How long was she gone?" None of those seemed like the most pressing questions, but he was having trouble wrapping his mind around a parent leaving their child unattended and vulnerable.

"It was around eleven, the mother said that she was only gone for a few minutes, but it was long enough for Marcus King to see her, decide to grab her daughter and use whatever ruse he came up with to gain her trust long enough to take her."

"Dad in the picture?" He wasn't quite ready to accept this was

Marcus yet.

"They were never married. The dad has been in and out of the picture, but not by choice. The mother keeps taking the girl and disappearing. The father has been concerned that she hasn't been properly caring for the child, and given what's happened, I guess he was right."

"Possible custodial kidnapping then?"

"That's what the cops thought at first, but the father swears he doesn't have her. I know they all say that, but a white van was captured on security cameras around the bar at the time Payton was taken. At Chloe and Fin's house this morning, Marcus blew out my tires then drove off in a white van."

It wasn't a lot to go on, but for now, it didn't matter who had Payton. They would keep an eye on her father, and if Marcus King did have her, then they'd find her when they found Savannah.

"We need to go through Marcus's life with a fine-tooth comb and find out where's he's hiding. He hasn't surfaced in a year, yet he's got a car and a place to stay. Someone is supporting him. We just have to find out who that person is. Once we do, we'll find him, and then we'll find Savannah." Jett just hoped that wasn't going to be easier said than done.

* * * * *

1:45 P.M.

Revenge really was sweet.

Knowing that Chloe Luckman—or whatever her name was now—was no longer alive was like knowing that the last thing that held him tied to his past was gone. That chapter of his life was over, and it was now time to focus on a new one. A *better* one.

Marcus had it all worked out. He'd learned since the last time, and this time, he was going to do things differently. He didn't want to go back to prison.

It had been a mistake to kill the girls and dump their bodies.

If he hadn't, then the police would never have been on to him.

And he was going to have to be more careful about which girls he chose. Not that he intended to keep more than a handful at any one time. If he kept them alive, there would be no bodies; therefore, there would be nothing for the police to use against him. And if he took girls who might slip through the cracks, then he had even better odds of staying off the cops' radar.

Since he was going to be keeping the kids, then he needed someone to look after them.

Enter the blonde lady.

He didn't know her name yet; they hadn't had a chance to get acquainted. He was keeping her bound, gagged, blindfolded, and with earplugs in until he was ready for her. Keeping an adult was a completely different thing than keeping a child. The girl he would be able to manipulate, brainwash, and control—but the woman, he wasn't sure yet.

Marcus hadn't really been thinking about taking a woman right away. The plan had been to work on brainwashing the kid and then carefully choose a woman he thought he could manipulate into caring for the girls for him.

But then this woman had appeared.

He'd seen her exit the house with Chloe, and right away, he knew.

It was like a sign.

She was in a wheelchair. She couldn't walk, which had to mean that she was going to be easier to control than an able-bodied woman. So, he'd acted on gut instinct and brought her with him. It had almost gotten him caught, but everything had turned out okay.

Now he had a girl and a woman, and he wasn't altogether sure how to handle things. The woman may have been in a wheelchair, but she wasn't paralyzed; she was able to move her legs, and when he'd cut her with his knife to check whether she had feeling or not, she had cried out. Marcus didn't know what was wrong with her, and he didn't really care—all he cared about was that now he had exactly what he wanted, and he had all the time in the world to enjoy it.

Other than giving them a little water, he hadn't been in to see his new guests. He wanted them to spend some time alone and scared. Sometimes, the anticipation of what was coming next was scarier than the actual thing. He wanted to let their minds run wild as they imagined every horrible thing that he might have in store for them.

Perhaps it was time they got a little sneak peek.

The woman, at least.

He wasn't quite ready to touch the girl. For some reason, he felt weird about hurting her. Almost remorseful.

Marcus had never felt that way before.

What he did never bothered him.

Just like it hadn't bothered the people who had hurt him.

He wasn't sure how badly the girl had suffered, but at the very least, she had been neglected, so they had that in common. And it was the commonality that was throwing him.

Now wasn't the time to be getting emotionally invested. There was no way he could let the girl go; she had seen his face. Maybe he should just kill her quickly and be done with it, then go looking for a child who wasn't going to start engendering these feelings.

It wasn't like he had to decide right now—he had plenty of time, and if he decided to just kill the kid, he would make sure he didn't dump her body on the side of the road. Perhaps he could bury her here somewhere, or maybe he could chop the body up into pieces and dump her in the river, or even burn her—although he'd heard that fire needed to be over 1400 degrees Fahrenheit to burn up human bones. Marcus wasn't sure he could create a fire that hot without attracting unwanted attention.

Unlocking the door, he closed and locked it behind him. You

could never be too careful. Then he crossed the room and unlocked the second door. Because he was committed this time to making sure that he didn't get caught, he then went to a third door and unlocked it. This door led to a staircase, at the bottom of which was door number four.

Behind it was the room.

He had taken months building it himself. Making sure it was soundproofed and well equipped. He intended for the girls he got and the woman who would care for them to live down here, so it needed everything. There was a bathroom, a small kitchenette, TV and toys, and books for the children to play with, a bed, and a table and chairs. This would be their home. At least until they were completely under his control, then he might consider moving them to the main house.

When he opened the last door, he had to do a double take.

Not because anything was wrong, but because everything was exactly as it had been when he'd left.

It was like time down here had stood still while it continued to tick by in the real world.

The little girl was huddled in the same corner he'd put her in when he had carried her down here. The woman lay against the opposite wall; she was on her side, her arms still behind her back, and the blindfold, gag and earplugs all still in place. The child had also kept her blindfold on, despite not being restrained in any way. He guessed his threats had worked.

He really was going to have to do something about their blue eyes.

Marcus bypassed the child, who shrank farther into the corner when she heard his footsteps and went to the woman. He had needs that had to be satisfied and right now, he didn't want to use the kid to get them met.

"Hello, beautiful," he said as he squatted at the woman's side and pulled out the earplugs.

She started at his touch and pressed back against the wall. She mumbled something through the gag, but he couldn't make out what it was.

"You have something you want to tell me?" When she nodded vigorously, he removed the gag.

"My boyfriend is an FBI agent," she said as soon as she could talk. Her voice was dry and croaky after spending so long with a rag stuffed in her mouth.

"That's nice for him," he replied, amused. He liked her already.

"I'm Chloe's best friend. She's an FBI agent too; they're going to do whatever it takes to find you."

"Let them try," he said confidently. No one would think to look for him here. Why would they? There was no reason to think that he would have come here to find a safe haven.

"They won't stop looking for me. Ever," she added for emphasis.

He leaned in close until he knew she could feel his breath against her skin even if she couldn't see him. "They can look all they want, but they won't find you. Ever," he added for his own emphasis.

To her credit, she didn't flinch. "What are you going to do with me?"

"I'm going to keep you, use you however I want." He trailed a hand down her shoulder, along her arm, to her hip. He left it there, letting his touch and his words sink in.

"Wh-what about the girl?" she asked, the first crack in her composure showing. She was a tough one—he liked that. He would definitely enjoy their time together.

"I'm not sure yet," he answered honestly. If they were going to live together, then he needed to gain her trust, and to do that, he thought it would be better to be truthful wherever possible.

This surprised her. "Let her go."

"I can't do that. She saw my face."

"She won't tell."

They both knew she would. It was inevitable. Several of the

children he'd had the pleasure of spending time with had begged to go home to their parents, promising that they wouldn't say anything, but both he and they had known it was a lie.

Marcus was done talking.

He was ready to have a little fun.

He bent to pick her up, then yelped in pain as something buried itself deep into his shoulder.

* * * * *

2:19 P.M.

"Payton, run!" Savannah screamed as she plunged the knife into Marcus King's shoulder. It wasn't a sharp knife; there hadn't been much in the drawers, so they'd had to work with what they could get.

When they'd heard footsteps earlier, she'd had Payton put the blindfold, gag, and earplugs back in so Marcus didn't know they had been communicating. It had worked. Marcus had given them both some water and then left.

The second the door closed behind him, she counted to one thousand and then thumped the floor to get Payton to come back over. The girl had been able to find a pair of scissors in the art supplies that were in the toy box, and although they were fairly blunt, Savannah had been able to saw through her binds. She'd cut herself several times along the way, and her biggest fear was that Marcus would have noticed before she was ready.

Once free, she had armed herself with a knife from the drawers in the kitchenette and then they had put their blindfolds and her gag and earplugs back on, then she'd put her arms behind her back, and they'd waited.

And waited.

And waited.

It had felt like an eternity.

Lying here, her bad hip aching, her head throbbing, she had prayed that he would hurry up and return. Now that he was here, she almost wished she was back to the waiting.

Without letting go of the knife, she yanked it out of his flesh and swung it down again, this time connecting with his arm as instinct had him throwing it up to protect himself.

"Payton, run and don't stop, not for anything," she called out again, ripping off her blindfold. Marcus had surprised her by saying that he wasn't sure what he wanted to do about the child, and she hoped that indecision would be enough for him to not really worry about her running. Something about Payton had confused him. If Savannah had to guess, it was because the girl had clearly been neglected. Maybe Marcus could empathize with her because, as a child, he had been neglected or abused as well. Maybe she could use that to her advantage.

When she swung the knife a third time, he finally reacted enough to stop her.

Just as she had hoped, he paid no attention to Payton; Savannah was the focus of his attention right now. The focus of his rage.

The calm and in control man who had been talking to her just moments ago was gone. Now a raging bull was in his place. Marcus's face went bright red, and his eyes clouded over with anger. He swung a fist at her and connected with her jaw, sending her head snapping violently to the side.

"How dare you," he screamed as his hands clamped painfully hard on her shoulders, and he shook her roughly.

Savannah really hoped she knew what she was doing.

The plan was that Payton ran, got away, and got help, but she hadn't thought in too much detail what Marcus was going to do to her while Payton ran.

It looked like she was about to find out.

Or maybe there was a way she could escape too.

The keys were in his pocket. All she had to do was get ahold of them, incapacitate him enough to buy her time to get to the door and lock it behind her. Then she'd be safe, and Marcus would be trapped here until Jett could come and arrest him.

She forced herself to go limp, and Marcus immediately loosened his grip, believing her to have passed out.

The knife was still in her hand, and this time instead of aiming high, she aimed low and shoved the blade into his stomach.

Marcus screamed, his hands releasing her to clutch at the knife embedded in his abdomen.

Taking advantage, Savannah reached into his pocket, her fingers curling around the keys. He batted at her hands, but his were covered in blood now and slippery.

She had the keys in her hand.

All she had to do was get to the door.

Now more than ever, she wished she hadn't let her fears cripple her, and she'd gotten out of her wheelchair and started walking.

With adrenalin buzzing in her system and affording her extra strength, Savannah tried to struggle to her feet.

She didn't make it.

After twelve months of not being used, her legs gave out, and she collapsed.

That gave Marcus enough time to get ahold of her.

He snatched her around the waist, picked her up and carried her to the bed, tossing her on it like she was nothing more than an irritating gnat.

Stalking over to the toy box, he rifled through it, throwing things out left, right and center.

Savannah wasn't sure what she should do. Should she try to make another run for it and infuriate him further, or should she just give up and wait for him to come back?

Her body made its own choice.

It just wasn't in her to give up.

She swung her legs over the edge of the mattress and tried to push herself into a standing position.

"You aren't going anywhere." Marcus's arm connected with her chest, knocking her backward as she was halfway to standing. Placing one of his tree trunk-like arms across her stomach, he held her in place as he took hold of one of her wrists and wrapped the string around it then tied it to the bedpost. He repeated this with her other arm and both her legs until she was bound, spread eagle, to the bed.

She had never felt more vulnerable in her life.

The only saving grace was that she was still fully clothed in the jeans and magenta sweater she'd put on this morning.

This morning.

It was hard to believe that just this morning, her life had been completely normal and looking brighter than it had in years, and now she might actually be dead before the day was over.

At least if she was about to die, she had spent her last night making love to the man of her dreams and then slept wrapped up in his arms. She wasn't sure she could have planned a better night if she had known it would be her last.

Her one regret was that she hadn't told Jett that she loved him.

If she could go back and do it over, then she would make sure she said those three little words.

Because bad luck found her at every turn, Marcus stood over her, bloodied and almost manic looking with a pair of scissors in his hand. Ironically, they were the same pair of scissors that she and Payton had used to saw through the zip ties that bound her wrists together.

"You don't get to wear clothes," he said, snipping the scissors in her face before going to work cutting her clothes off her. The way he said it was odd like he was parroting back something that had been said to him. Maybe he really had been abused as a child.

She wanted to try to get him talking—anything that might buy her time while Payton got help—but she was afraid that anything she said would only have the opposite effect and antagonize him more.

"This is your fault," he snarled as he tossed the last of her clothes on the floor, leaving her completely naked and one hundred percent at his mercy. "You made me angry. I can't be held responsible for my actions."

"Like it was Chloe's fault that you went to prison even though you were the one who raped and killed all those poor little girls."

He slapped her. "Your friend should have kept her mouth shut. She deserved what she got."

"What you did to her wasn't in a fit of rage. You threatened her in court, and you planned it out and bided your time to come for her. You killed her in cold blood."

Marcus put his hand on her face and pinched her cheeks together. "You should keep your mouth shut too. You're mine now." Still holding her face with one hand, his other moved to her breast, kneading it painfully hard. Then he put his hand between her legs and shoved his fingers inside of her, making her entire body clench as though it could force him out. He leaned in close, so his breath was hot against her face. "Every. Single. Inch of you. So, get ideas of escaping out of your head. I'm going to teach you a lesson, then I'm going to go and get the kid, then we're going to spend some time getting to know each other."

He removed his hand and went to the bathroom.

He clearly wasn't worried about Payton.

It was like he knew she wasn't going to be able to escape.

She had failed.

She and Payton were stuck here forever.

Jett might find her, but he just as easily might not.

This could be her life now.

The room, being raped and tortured until she angered Marcus enough that he killed her.

"I'm sorry, Jett," she whispered aloud.

"You'll be sorry, all right," Marcus snapped, appearing above her again with a washcloth and a bucket of water in his hands.

Savannah fought against her bonds even though she knew she wasn't going anywhere, and all she got for her troubles was burning pain in her wrists and ankles as the string cut through her skin.

Marcus paid no attention to her squirming, he just laid the towel over her face, and Savannah felt her whole body go still.

He was going to waterboard her.

She'd heard about it.

It could kill people.

Stay calm, stay calm, stay calm, she repeated the mantra over and over in her head.

But the second the water hit her face, any semblance of calm disappeared, and she dropped completely into a dark pit of shock and horror.

* * * * *

3:00 P.M.

"Next right," Tom told him as he drove as fast as was safe in this primarily family-filled neighborhood.

This was not the kind of neighborhood where you'd expect to find a neighbor holding someone hostage, but Jett believed this was exactly where Marcus King was hiding out.

They had gone through every single person who'd ever been a part of Marcus's life, however small, with a fine-tooth comb trying to find anyone who might have been persuaded to take pity on Marcus and help him.

There had been only one person who stood out.

Now he and Tom were heading there as fast as they could. He needed to get to Savannah—the longer she was with him, the greater the chances that Marcus was going to hurt her.

That he still couldn't figure out why Marcus had taken her in the first place was driving him insane. Marcus should have just shot her and run. Well, not *should have.* If Marcus had killed Savannah, then his life would have effectively been over. But it would have made a lot more sense than kidnapping her. What did he want with an adult victim? His preference was preteen girls. And if he really had been the one who abducted Payton Zubriski, what was he going to do with two victims? That was going to be a lot to handle, and Marcus wasn't used to handling victims. His previous MO had been to kidnap, rape, then strangle them and dump their bodies.

Although Jett was trying not to think too much about that.

Because if Marcus had stuck with that part of his MO, then Savannah could already be dead.

Right now, he had to believe that everything to do with Marcus's previous MO was out the window, and they were playing with a whole new set of rules. Which was both unnerving and reassuring.

Jett was about to ask Tom something when a child suddenly darted out between two cars in the middle of the road.

Tom slammed on the brakes, and they screeched to a halt, stopping mere inches from the little girl.

A redheaded girl with a dirty, tear-stained face, and a patched jacket.

Payton Zubriski.

Both he and Tom jumped from the vehicle. "Payton?" Jett asked as they approached the girl slowly.

She froze, her eyes darting back and forth between the two of them, weighing up her options. He hoped she didn't run—he didn't want to have to restrain the child by force, but they needed to know if she had been taken by Marcus King if he still had Savannah with him, and where she'd come from.

"It's okay, Payton. We're police officers." Tom stopped where he was and got down on his knees, so he was eye to eye with the girl.

That seemed to reassure her, and she stayed put.

"My name's Tom. We've been looking for you." Tom gave the girl an easy smile. Jett hung back, letting Tom deal with the child since he seemed to have already begun building a rapport.

"M-my mom, she wasn't really hurt, was she?" Payton asked in a small voice.

"No, she wasn't, honey. Did your daddy take you last night, Payton?" Tom asked.

"No." The girl shook her head, making her messy red braids whip about her head. "I haven't seen him in ages. Not since my mom and I moved."

"He missed you." Tom tentatively reached out a hand and rested it on her shoulder.

"I missed him too. Can I go see him?"

"You can, but first, do you know who the man is who took you?"

"Savannah said his name was Marcus King and that he was going to hurt us if we didn't get away."

Savannah.

She'd at least been alive long enough to help the child escape, but what had Marcus done to her for it?

"How did you get away?" Jett asked, dropping down beside Tom.

"We tricked him. We pretended that Savannah was still tied up, but she wasn't. We found a knife, and she stabbed him. Then she told me to run. The door was locked, so I had to climb out a window," Payton explained disjointedly. He didn't need to know everything right now, and it didn't need to make sense. He just needed to know where they were.

"Take us to the house," he ordered.

Tom shot him a small frown, but Payton nodded readily. "Savannah said I should get help, that was my job. I wanted to help her fight him, but she said that if I wanted to help, this was what I had to do." The girl looked pleased to be fulfilling her roll in their plan.

Payton led them between two houses and into the next block. She didn't hesitate before leading them straight to a large blue and gray Craftsman house. There was a row of rose bushes that would make a gorgeous show of color when in bloom, and a large swing on the porch. Evil was hiding behind a pretty veneer.

"Down there." Payton pointed down the driveway to a large shed down the back of the property.

"We'll call in backup," Tom said, pulling out his phone.

"I'm not waiting." Savannah was in there. And Marcus was going to be angry, so there was no way Jett was waiting. Waiting could be signing Savannah's death warrant.

"Check the house," he called over his shoulder as he pulled out his gun and headed for the shed.

"Jett," Tom called after him, but he was already getting into the zone.

Payton had said that the door was locked, so he bypassed it to find the window she had come through. When he located it, he approached carefully. He didn't want to alert Marcus to his presence until he was ready.

The inside of the shed was just that.

A shed.

It was empty aside from the tools and things scattered about, but there was an open door over in one corner.

Easing the window farther open, Jett climbed inside.

The place was mostly quiet, but he thought he could hear muffled sounds coming from somewhere.

Quietly, he crept across the floor to the door, easing it open to find himself in another room. This one was completely empty, but the muffled sounds grew louder. He was getting closer.

A hand closed over his shoulder, and instinct had him spinning around, gun raised, ready to use it.

And found Tom.

"What are you doing here?" he hissed.

"I'm not letting you go in there alone. I locked Payton in the car and told her to stay there till officers came to get her."

"I think they're down there." He gestured to the other door.

Tom nodded, and together they made their way to door number three. When he swung it open, light flooded up from a room at the bottom of a short staircase.

"You've had enough, have you?" a voice snarled. "Maybe next time, you'll think twice before crossing me."

If Tom hadn't wrapped an arm around his bicep, Jett probably would have gone barreling down there.

Marcus was punishing Savannah.

Clinging to control, they took the stairs slowly, but that control fled when they reached the bottom, and he saw what was going on.

Savannah was naked on the bed, restrained, a wet towel on her face.

Marcus stood above her with a bucket in his hands.

"Move away from her," Jett growled.

"So, you're the FBI boyfriend." Marcus turned slowly, not lowering the bucket, which was positioned directly above Savannah's face. Jett saw blood on his shirt, his arm, and his leg. Savannah had hurt him. His heart swelled with pride for his girl. Now, if she could just hold on a few more minutes, he'd do his part and get her out of here.

The temptation to kill Marcus for laying a hand on the woman he loved didn't diminish. But Jett didn't know how much water was in the bucket, and he didn't know how much Savannah had already swallowed. She wasn't moving, and she hadn't indicated that she knew he was here. If Marcus poured the remaining water on her, she could drown.

For the moment, he would take things slow and try talking Marcus down, but if that failed, he wouldn't hesitate to shoot.

"How did you get your father to agree to let you hide out here?"

Marcus seemed surprised by the question but complied with an answer. "He felt sorry for me. For not being around when I was a kid. For what my mother did to me."

"What did she do to you, Marcus?"

"What you think she did."

"She was a drug addict, she sold you for drug money."

Marcus shrugged. "It's not an uncommon story."

"That doesn't make it okay."

Darkness crept over Marcus's face, and Jett saw the man who had raped and strangled at least a dozen children—that they knew of. "I got my revenge."

"On little girls who did nothing to you."

"You don't know what it was like for me." Marcus's face contorted into a mask of venom.

"I know what pain is like. We all do. That's not an excuse for what you did. You want my sympathy? You don't have it. My sympathy goes to the child version of you. The one who suffered something horrific that no child should ever have to. But you? You get nothing. You chose to do this. You don't deserve anyone's sympathy."

"I don't want your sympathy; I want your blood."

Marcus dropped his hand to his waist.

Jett didn't hesitate.

He fired.

* * * * *

3:30 P.M.

"Is she alive?"

The words floated above her like distinct entities of their own. They sparkled, each a different color, and danced in front of her eyes. They flew to the left, then wobbled back to the right, then began to spin in circles, faster and faster, until she was so dizzy, Savannah thought she was going to throw up.

The heavy weight that had been crushing her head suddenly disappeared.

Then something tickled across her neck.

"She is, but we need an ambulance. Now."

An ambulance?

Who needed an ambulance?

She needed an ambulance?

Savannah wasn't sure of anything.

She felt groggy and disoriented. Her mind had kind of checked out when the first drops of water began to soak the towel on her face and slowly begin to smother her.

When the water hit her throat, it felt like she was drowning.

She knew that feeling.

When she was six, she'd been on a family vacation at the beach. She and Sawyer had been in the water, riding on kickboards, when she'd gotten caught in a riptide. She was a good swimmer, and she tried to swim against it, but it was like swimming while being cocooned in concrete.

Not only hadn't she been able to get back to the shore, but inch by inch, she was being dragged out to sea.

Her little legs had gotten so tired, she could barely kick with them anymore.

Then the panic set in.

She had been convinced that she was going to drown.

As soon as she thought it was going to happen, it did.

A huge wave knocked her under and tossed her about until she wasn't sure which way was up and which was down.

Water began to flood her mouth and her nose.

The world became nothing but water. It surrounded her, filled her, and it was soon to be her coffin.

Then strong arms had snaked around her, and she had been dragged up into the fresh air.

She'd been saved then.

And she'd been saved now.

"The string is embedded in her skin."

The voice tore her concentration away from drowning and death.

"She must have been thrashing about so much it dug into her flesh."

"We should just cut the string from around the bedposts. Let the doctors at the hospital remove it where it's stuck in her wrists and ankles."

A moment later, the tension in her limbs released.

"Savannah? Can you hear me?"

Someone's hand was on her jaw, and her face was tilted to the side.

Her eyes were open.

Maybe?

She thought so.

She could see a face above her, but it was blurry like she was underwater.

The next thing she knew, she was floating.

Although, it was kind of bumpy floating.

No, not floating.

Being carried.

"Savannah, talk to me. Please. You're scaring me."

Scared?

She wasn't scared anymore. She wasn't quite sure what she was.

"Savannah." Her name was said like a plea.

Lips brushed across hers, so lightly she thought she might have imagined them, but then they pressed harder, kissing her as though she were Sleeping Beauty, and a kiss was all that would wake her.

By some miracle, her mind began to clear.

Along with it, her senses returned.

She was in a room, smaller and darker than the room where she had almost lost her life. She was wrapped in something that was warm and soft against her icy skin. She hurt, mostly her wrists and ankles, but her head and chest too. Her cheek rested on something bony, a shoulder, and she could see the profile of whoever's arms she was cradled in.

Jett.

Jett was here.

Relief flooded through her.

"I love you." The words seemed to tumble out of her mouth of their own accord. As part of her was still afraid that if she didn't say them quickly enough, she would never get another chance.

"I love you, too, sweetheart." Jett smiled down at her, then sank down to sit on the floor, settling her on his lap and holding her so tightly it almost hurt. Not that she would ask him to loosen his grip for anything.

Now that the I love yous were out of the way, she had to know. "I'm sorry. Are you angry with me?"

"Angry with you?" His green eyes were confused, and one of his hands began to rhythmically stroke the length of her spine. She suspected the gesture was intended to soothe and reassure them both.

"I broke my promise." She was crying now. It seemed she couldn't get away from water no matter what.

"Shh, it's all right." Jett clutched her tighter, kissing away her tears.

No.

It wasn't all right.

He had asked only one thing of her, and she hadn't given it to him.

"I promised I wouldn't put myself in danger again, but I did. Marcus shot Chloe, and he was going to shoot her again. I had to stop him. I yelled out. I didn't know he was going to take me. I'm sorry." Savannah thought she might be babbling incoherently, but Jett appeared to be following along.

"And if you hadn't stopped him from firing that second shot, then she and her baby would probably be dead."

She looked up at him through her tears. "They're alive?"

Jett kissed her forehead. "Both alive and doing well."

Savannah sagged against Jett's chest. Chloe and the baby were okay. Even if she had died here, at least they would have lived.

"Sweetheart, did Marcus—did he—did he rape you?" Jett asked tightly.

"No. He, just—he was angry I tried to help Payton escape—his fingers," she was back to babbling, and a new wave of tears crashed down upon her.

"Shh, it's okay. You're okay. It'll be okay," Jett buried his face in her hair and whispered the same string of consolations over and over again.

Was she really okay?

Was everything really going to be okay?

Right now, it was hard to believe.

So much had happened in the last few days.

She felt weird—all churned up inside and completely unlike herself.

Shock, she supposed.

Maybe once it wore off, things would look better.

At least, however bad things were, she had Jett. She just had to cling to that. He would be her anchor. When her world was all messed up, and she felt tossed about and unsure of her footing and which direction to take, she could lean on him.

Savannah turned her face into his chest and let the tidal wave of sobs that had been steadily building inside her break free.

* * * * *

8:28 P.M.

"I really would have felt better if you'd stayed in the hospital tonight," Jett told Savannah for probably the fortieth time since they'd left the hospital about fifteen minutes ago.

"I am not spending another Christmas in the hospital," Savannah replied.

As far as he was concerned, that was not a good reason to have discharged herself.

"I'm okay, Jett—really." She gave him a tired smile.

She was right. Physically, she was all right. The wounds on her wrists and ankles were nasty, but they'd been treated and bandaged. They'd heal, although they would leave scars that would be a constant reminder of her ordeal. It wasn't how she was doing physically that he was worried about; it was how she was doing psychologically.

Savannah had been attacked, lost her home and nearly died in a fire, then she'd been kidnapped, sexually assaulted, and tortured. No one could be okay after that.

"Jett, please," she said when he opened his mouth. "I know you're worried about me, and all right, I'm probably not *okay*, but I will be. I just need some time."

"You have time, sweetheart." He reached out and brushed a lock of hair off her cheek, tucking it behind her ear. "You have all the time in the world."

She smiled at him again and rested her head back against the headrest. She hadn't slept at the hospital, just waited anxiously for doctors to do their tests and tend to her wounds. No matter how many times he told her to lie down and close her eyes, she had refused.

"I'll have you back to my place soon, then you can get some rest," he told her.

"I'm too wired to sleep," she said, fidgeting with the edge of one of the white bandages wrapped around her wrist. She'd been fidgeting ever since they'd arrived at the hospital. He knew she was dwelling on something—he just wasn't sure which something it was, and he didn't want to push her right now.

He pulled to a stop in his driveway and came around to Savannah's side to pick her up and carry inside. "If you don't want to sleep just yet, how about we make your gingerbread carousel?"

She wrapped her arms around his neck. "We can't. Even if I wanted to, everything I had to make it was destroyed along with the rest of my house."

Balancing her in one arm as he unlocked the front door, he said, "Well, I thought you might not want to sleep, knowing how stubborn you can be." She huffed a small chuckle at his teasing. "So, while you were at the hospital, I asked Hannah to find everything you would need to make your gingerbread creation. It's your Christmas tradition; let me do it with you."

Jett had half expected an argument, but instead, Savannah just grinned. "You really did that for me? Asked Hannah to go and find everything I'd need just so I could bake tonight?"

"Of course." He kissed her temple. "You know I'd do anything for you, Savannah." He paused in the hall. "Not being able to be there for you when I knew you needed me is one of the hardest things I've ever had to do. But from here on out, you're my number one, okay?"

She kissed his cheek. "Okay."

"I want you to do something for me. Do you trust me?"

"Yes," she replied, with only the merest hint of hesitation.

"I want you to try to walk."

She dipped her head, so her eyes were focused on the floor and not on his face. "I already tried. In Marcus's basement. I tried to run after I stabbed him, and I tried to run while he was in the bathroom, but I couldn't," she finished softly.

"You can. Even if you don't believe in yourself, I believe in you. I'm not expecting you to be able to walk perfectly in one night, but just try a couple of steps. You can do this, Savannah."

"Do you really think so, or are you just trying to make me feel better?"

If she didn't have any faith in herself right now, then he was happy to share his faith in her. "I don't *think* you can do it—I *know* you can."

"I've been doing my exercises. The ones I learned in physical therapy last time," she admitted.

"You have?" He was surprised and yet not surprised to hear that.

"I was just afraid to try walking."

"Afraid of what?"

"Failing, I guess. It was easier to just not try walking and never know if I could or not than to get my hopes up, try, and fail."

"You're not going to fail." Jett kept his arm around her waist but lowered her legs, so her feet were touching the floor. "You can do this," he said again.

Savannah nodded but didn't look convinced.

"Why don't you try walking to the kitchen door? It's only about four or five steps."

"You'll stay right beside me?"

"Every step of the way."

"Okay." Savannah took a deep breath and readied herself.

When she nodded, he slowly released his hold on her until she was standing on her own two feet.

"I'm doing it." She grinned.

"You sure are." He grinned back. He couldn't be prouder of her. Everyone had fears—it was overcoming them that was the important thing. "Now, try taking a step."

Keeping her arms out for balance, Savannah lifted her bad leg and swung it forward, wincing at the movement, then brought her good leg up to meet it. "I did it. I took a step," she squealed excitedly.

Jett moved a couple of feet away. "Come to me, honey." He held his arms open, ready to catch her if she fell.

Concentrating just like a toddler taking their very first steps, Savannah took another step, and then another, and then another until she reached him and threw herself into his arms. "I was walking," she said as though she couldn't quite believe it, fresh tears brimming in her eyes.

"Again?" He caught a fat, round tear as it snaked its way down her cheek. "I don't even have to ask if these are happy tears. I already know they are."

"Thank you. For everything. For giving us—for giving me—a second chance, for saving me in the fire, for saving me today, for giving me the courage I needed to try walking again. I love you, Jett Crane. You're my Christmas miracle."

"You got it all wrong, babe. *You* are *my* Christmas miracle."

Jett lifted her off her feet and kissed her like both of their dreams had just come true.

DECEMBER 25TH

2:44 A.M.

"You have flour all over your face." Jett laughed.

Savannah brushed at her cheek with a flour-dusted hand. She always got dirty when she baked. She added one last little dot of icing then gave the work an appraising glance. She probably could have done a better job if she wasn't hurt, and she'd had more time, but all in all, it looked pretty good.

"Finished," she announced.

They both stood back and surveyed the gingerbread carousel.

It spun like a real carousel, and she'd decorated it in pinks, purples, and blues—her favorite colors. The little horses were cute, with flowing icing manes, and beautifully colored saddles. They had also made a few little gingerbread people to ride the carousel. They'd even made a gingerbread Christmas tree—not because it had anything to do with the carousel but because it was Christmas Eve, and she was excited.

"I can't believe you made that." Jett slipped an arm around her waist and pulled her back to rest against him.

"*We* made that," she corrected him.

"You did most of the work."

"We made it together," she insisted.

"Okay, together," Jett agreed. "I like doing things together with you," he whispered in her ear.

"Very subtle, Jett," she giggled.

"Hey, it's Christmas Day, can you blame me for wanting to celebrate by being in bed with my girl?"

"It's Christmas Day?" she glanced at the clock on Jett's kitchen wall. She'd been having so much fun that she completely lost track of time.

"For a couple of hours now."

"We better get cleaning; we made such a mess." There were dirty bowls, beaters, dish towels, spatulas, flour, icing, and mess spread out over nearly every inch of counter and table space.

"Leave it." Jett turned the chair she was sitting in around to face him.

"It's all dirty," she protested.

"We can clean it later. Right now, I just want to enjoy you." He kissed her softly, slowly, sensuously, until her whole world tunneled down and existed of nothing but her and Jett and this kiss.

Her hands went to his shirt, and she began to undo the buttons. She was halfway done when he suddenly clamped his hands around hers, stilling them.

"I have something for you."

"Jett," she groaned. He couldn't kiss her like that then completely change track.

"Let's go to the living room." He didn't wait for her consent, just picked her up and carried her to the living room, setting her down on the couch and turning on the lights covering the fireplace and the Christmas tree.

While Jett started a fire, her gaze went to the Christmas tree. It was so pretty and sparkly, the tinsel glistened in the glow from the fairy lights, the decorations sparkled. It made her think of her own tree, which was gone now, along with everything else she owned.

Before the grief of her loss could overwhelm her, she noticed a box wrapped in gingerbread house wrapping paper sitting under the tree. "There are gifts under there."

"Santa must have visited while we were baking."

Savannah rolled her eyes. "You got me something. When did you have time?"

"I actually bought it last year." Jett retrieved the box and joined her on the sofa. "When you were in the hospital. I wanted to come and see you, I just wasn't sure you were in a place where you were ready to take me back."

He was right. If he'd approached her last year and told her he wanted her back, she would have thrown him out.

No questions, no explanations, nothing.

She would've just told him to go.

She'd been in a dark place then, but now there was light shining down on her.

"I hope you like it."

Jett handed her the box, and she carefully removed the wrapping paper—she was one of those wrapping paper savers— and then opened the box. Inside was an album and a smaller box.

"Open the album first," Jett said.

She did and gasped when she saw what was inside.

It was photos of her and Sawyer as kids with their parents. There was the day they were born, the day they'd come home from the hospital, sitting in high chairs eating solids for the first time, first steps, first day of school, family vacations. Memories of times when her family had been whole and happy.

She'd had family photo albums in her house, and photos on her laptop and her phone, but she'd lost all of them in the fire.

"How did you get these?" she asked, her eyes growing watery.

"I forgot how much you cry over everything." Jett smiled and tenderly held a finger to her cheek to catch her tears. "I called Sawyer while we were at the hospital and asked him to make copies of all the family photos he had."

She had never been so touched by a gift before. "Thank you for doing this for me." She took Jett's face in her hands and kissed him.

"Of course."

Since the photo album clearly wasn't what he had bought for her last year, she eagerly opened the smaller box and gave another gasp when she opened it.

"Oh, Jett, it's beautiful," she gushed as she removed the bracelet from the jewelry box. It was a charm bracelet, and each little charm was made to look like gingerbread. There was a gingerbread man and a gingerbread woman, a gingerbread house, a gingerbread tree, and a gingerbread heart. "I love it."

"You do?" Jett looked slightly unsure.

"I do. I love it. Will you put it on me?" Savannah held out the bracelet and her wrist.

"You sure it won't hurt your wounds?"

"I don't care. I want to wear it." When Jett had put the bracelet on, she pointed to an envelope sitting on the table by the door. "Can you get that? It's for you."

"For me?" Jett looked confused.

"You weren't the only one who asked Hannah for a favor."

Jett collected the envelope then sat back down with her to open it. He pulled out a single piece of paper and then glanced from it to her. "This is the cabin we stayed in, where I made you the decoration."

"It's yours," she told him gleefully.

"Mine?" he asked, shocked.

"The money I inherited from my parents was just sitting in bank accounts. I'd been wanting to do something with it, so I bought it. Well, everything has to be finalized, but I spoke to the owner, and he accepted my offer. This place is yours."

"Savannah, this is too much."

"No, it's not. You are always doing stuff for other people, you're always taking care of them and looking after them. Well, this is for you. It's a place where you can go when you need you time. Where you can relax and hang out and just chill."

"We," he corrected. "Where *we* can relax and hang out and just chill. Savannah, this is the most amazing gift anyone has ever given me."

"We have a whole new life ahead of us now. A life together." After her father had died, she'd felt like she'd never have a real family again. Then Jett had come into her life the first time, and she'd started to believe that maybe she could. But then she'd ruined things. As unlikely as it was, she'd been given a second chance, and this time she was going to keep ahold of it with both hands.

"Okay, now we get some sleep," Jett announced, moving to gather her up.

"Can we sleep down here?"

"Down here?"

"In front of the tree. I want to feel all Christmassy. This time last year, I was stuck in a hospital bed, in so much pain, I could barely think, and I thought I'd never walk again. This year, I want to enjoy every single second of Christmas—and of you."

"That, I think we can manage."

Jett turned off the main light, but left on the Christmas lights, then helped her lie down on the couch before stretching out beside her, holding her close against his side.

This was pretty close to perfection.

Lying surrounded by twinkling fairy lights and a roaring fire, wrapped up in the arms of the man she loved, she felt complete.

Content, she finally allowed exhaustion to take hold, and her eyes fluttered closed, sleep already claiming her.

"Merry Christmas, Jett."

Lips touched the top of her head. "Merry Christmas, Savannah."

Happy, she drifted off to sleep.

Jane has loved reading and writing since she can remember. She writes dark and disturbing crime/mystery/suspense with some romance thrown in because, well, who doesn't love romance?! She has several series including the complete Detective Parker Bell series, the Count to Ten series, the Christmas Romantic Suspense series, and the Flashes of Fate series of novelettes.

When she's not writing Jane loves to read, bake, go to the beach, ski, horse ride, and watch Disney movies. She has a black belt in Taekwondo, a 200+ collection of teddy bears, and her favorite color is pink. She has the world's two most sweet and pretty Dalmatians, Ivory and Pearl. Oh, and she also enjoys spending time with family and friends!

To connect and keep up to date please visit any of the following

Amazon – http://www.amazon.com/author/janeblythe
BookBub – https://www.bookbub.com/authors/jane-blythe
Email – mailto:janeblytheauthor@gmail.com
Facebook – http://www.facebook.com/janeblytheauthor
Goodreads – http://www.goodreads.com/author/show/6574160.Jane_Blythe
Instagram – http://www.instagram.com/jane_blythe_author
Reader Group – http://www.facebook.com/groups/janeskillersweethearts
Twitter – http://www.twitter.com/jblytheauthor
Website – http://www.janeblythe.com.au

sic enim dilexit Deus mundum ut Filium suum unigenitum daret ut omnis qui credit in eum habeat vitam aeternam

Printed in the USA
CPSIA information can be obtained
at www.ICGtesting.com
LVHW032253010823
754123LV00038B/260